GHOST BEACH

Look for more Goosebumps books
by R.L. Stine:

Goosebumps

GHOST BEACH

R.L. STINE

AN
APPLE
PAPERBACK

SCHOLASTIC INC.
New York Toronto London Auckland Sydney

A PARACHUTE PRESS BOOK

ISBN 0-590-47744-7

21 20 19 18 17 16 15 14   6 7 8 9/9

Printed in the U.S.A.   40

First Scholastic printing, August 1994

1

I don't remember how we got to the graveyard.

I remember the sky grew dark — and we were there.

My sister Terri and I walked past rows of crooked, old tombstones, cracked and covered with moss. Even though it was summer, a damp, gray fog had settled on everything, sending a chill through the air.

I shivered and pulled my jacket closer. "Wait up, Terri!" I called. As usual, she had plowed ahead. Graveyards get her all excited. "Where are you?" I yelled.

I squinted into the gray fog. I could see her shadowy figure up ahead, stopping every few seconds to examine a tombstone.

I read the words on the tombstone tilted at my feet:

In memory of John,
son of Daniel and Sarah Knapp,
who died March 25, 1766,
aged 12 years and 22 days.

Weird, I thought. That kid was about my age when he died. I turned twelve in February. The same month Terri turned eleven.

I hurried on. A sharp wind swept in. I searched the rows of old graves for my sister. She had disappeared into the thick fog. "Terri? Where did you go?" I called.

Her voice floated back to me. "I'm over here, Jerry."

"Where?" I pushed forward through the mist and the leaves. The wind swirled around me.

From nearby came a long, low howl. "Must be a dog," I murmured aloud.

The trees rattled their leaves at me. I shivered.

"Jer-ry." Terri's voice sounded a million miles away.

I walked a little further, then steadied myself against a tall tombstone. "Terri! Wait up! Stop moving around so much!"

I heard another long howl.

"You're going the wrong way," Terri called. "I'm over here."

"Great. Thanks a lot," I muttered. Why couldn't

I have a sister who liked baseball instead of exploring old cemeteries?

The wind made a deep sucking noise. A column of leaves, dust, and dirt swirled up in my face. I pinched my eyes shut.

When I opened them, I saw Terri crouched over a small grave. "Don't move," I called. "I'm coming."

I zigzagged my way around the tombstones until I reached her side. "It's getting dark," I said. "Let's get out of here."

I turned and took a step — and something grabbed my ankle.

I screamed and tried to pull away. But its grasp tightened.

A hand. Reaching up through the dirt beside the grave.

I let out a shrill scream. Terri screamed, too.

I kicked hard and broke free.

"Run!" Terri shrieked.

But I was already running.

As Terri and I stumbled over the wet grass, green hands popped up everywhere. *Thwack! Thwack! Thwack! Pop! Pop!*

The hands rose up. Reached for us. Grabbed at our ankles.

I darted to the left. *Thwack!* I dodged to the right. *Pop!*

"Run, Terri! Run!" I called to my sister. "Lift your knees!"

I could hear her sneakers pounding the ground behind me. Then I heard her terrified cry: "Jerry! They've got me!"

With a loud gasp, I spun around. Two big hands had wrapped themselves around her ankles.

I froze, watching my sister struggle.

"Jerry — help me! It won't let go!"

Taking a deep breath, I dove toward her. "Grab on to me," I instructed, holding out my arms.

I kicked at the two hands that held her.

Kicked as hard as I could. But they didn't move, didn't let go.

"I — I can't move!" Terri wailed.

The dirt seemed to shake at my feet. I peered down to see more hands sprouting up from the ground.

I tugged at Terri's waist. "Move!" I yelled frantically.

"I can't!"

"Yes, you can! You've got to keep trying!"

"Ohhh!" I let out a low cry as two hands grabbed *my* ankles.

Now I was caught.

We were both trapped.

2

"Jerry! What's your problem?" Terri asked.

I blinked. Terri stood beside me on a rocky strip of beach. I stared out at the calm ocean water beyond us and shook my head. "Wow. That was weird," I murmured. "I was remembering a bad dream I had a few months ago."

Terri frowned at me. "Why now?"

"It was about a cemetery," I explained. I turned back to glance at the tiny, old cemetery we'd just discovered at the edge of the pine woods behind us. "In my dream, green hands were popping out of the ground and grabbing our ankles."

"Gross," Terri replied. She brushed her dark brown bangs off her face. Except for the fact that she is one inch taller than me, we look like a perfect brother–sister combination. Same short brown hair, same freckles across our nose, same hazel eyes.

One difference: Terri has deep dimples in her cheeks when she smiles, and I don't. Thank goodness.

We walked along the ocean shore for a few minutes. Tall, gray boulders and scraggly pines stretched all the way to the water.

"Maybe you remembered that dream because you're nervous," Terri said thoughtfully. "You know. About being away from home for a whole month."

"Well, maybe," I agreed. "We've never been away this long. But what could happen here? Brad and Agatha are really great."

Brad Sadler is our distant cousin. *Ancient*, distant cousin is more like it. Dad said Brad and his wife, Agatha, were old when *he* was a kid!

But they're both fun, and really energetic despite their age. So when they invited us to come up to New England and spend the last month of summer with them in their old cottage near the beach, Terri and I eagerly said yes. It sounded great — especially since our only other choice was the cramped, hot apartment where we live in New Jersey.

We had arrived by train that morning. Brad and Agatha met us at the platform and drove us along the pine woods to the cottage.

After we had a chance to unpack and have some

lunch — big bowls of creamy clam chowder — Agatha said, "Now why don't you kids have a look around? There's lots to explore."

So here we were, checking things out. Terri grabbed my arm. "Hey, let's go back and check out that little cemetery!" she suggested eagerly.

"I don't know . . ." My frightening dream was still fresh in my mind.

"Oh, come on. There won't be any green hands. I promise. And I bet I can find some really cool gravestones for rubbings."

Terri loves exploring old graveyards. She loves all kinds of scary things. She reads scary mysteries by the dozen. And the weird thing is, she always reads the last chapter first.

Terri has to solve the mystery. She can't stand not knowing the answer.

My sister has a million interests, but gravestone rubbings is one of her stranger hobbies. She tapes a piece of rice paper over the gravestone inscription and then rubs the design onto the paper, using the side of a special wax crayon.

"Hey! Wait up," I called to her.

But Terri was already jogging up the beach toward the cemetery. "Come on, Jerry," she called. "Don't be a chicken."

I followed her off the beach and into the small forest. It smelled fresh and piney. The cemetery

7

was just inside, surrounded by a crumbly stone wall. We squeezed through the narrow opening in the wall that led inside.

Terri began inspecting the tombstones. "Wow. Some of these markers are really old," she announced. "Check out this one."

She pointed at a small gravestone. Engraved on the front was a skull with wings sprouting on either side of its head.

"It's a death's-head," my sister explained. "Very old Puritan symbol. Creepy, huh?" She read the inscription: " 'Here lies the body of Mr. John Sadler, who departed this life March 18, 1642, in the 38th year of his age.' "

"Sadler. Like us," I said. "Wow. I wonder if we're related." I did some quick calculations. "If we are, John Sadler is our great-great-great-great-grandsomething. He died over 350 years ago."

Terri had already moved on to another group of markers. "Here's one from 1647, and another from 1652. I don't think I've ever gotten rubbings this old before." She disappeared behind a tall tombstone.

I knew where *we'd* be spending the month. I'd had enough of cemeteries for today, though.

"Come on. Let's explore the beach, okay?" I checked around for Terri. "Terri? Where'd you go?" I stepped over to the tall tombstone.

Not there.

"Terri?" The ocean breeze rustled the pine branches above us. "Terri, cut it out, okay?"

I took a couple of steps. "You know I don't like this," I warned.

Terri's head popped up from behind a tombstone about ten feet away. "Why? You scared?"

I didn't like the grin on her face. "Who, me?" I said. "Never!"

Terri stood up. "Okay, chicken. But I'm coming back here tomorrow." She followed me out of the cemetery and onto the rocky beach.

"I wonder what's down here," I said, heading along the shoreline.

"Oh, look at this." Terri stooped to pluck a tiny yellow-and-white wildflower that had sprouted up between two large rocks. "Butter-and-eggs," she announced. "Weird name for a wildflower, huh?"

"Very," I agreed. Terri Sadler Hobby Number Two: wildflowers. She likes to collect them and press them in a huge cardboard contraption called a plant press.

Terri frowned. "*Now* what's your problem?"

"We keep stopping. I want to go exploring. Agatha said there's a small beach down here where we can go swimming if we want."

"Okay, okay," she replied, rolling her hazel eyes.

We trudged on until we reached a small, sandy beach. It was really more rock than sand. Staring out to the water, I saw a long rock jetty stretching out into the ocean.

"Wonder what that's for," Terri said.

"It helps hold the beach together," I explained. I was just about to launch into my explanation of beach erosion when Terri gasped.

"Jerry — look! Up there!" she cried. She pointed to a tall mound of rocks just past the jetty along the shoreline. Nestled high into the rocks, on top of a wide ledge, sat a large, dark cave.

"Let's climb up and explore it," Terri cried eagerly.

"No, wait!" I remembered what Mom and Dad had said to me that morning as we boarded the train: Keep an eye on Terri and don't let her get too carried away with things. "It might be dangerous," I said. I *am* the older brother, after all. And I'm the sensible one.

She made a face. "Give me a break," she muttered. Terri made her way across the beach and toward the cave. "At least let's get a closer look. We can ask Brad and Agatha later whether or not it's safe."

I followed behind her. "Yeah, right. Like ninety-year-olds ever go cave exploring."

10

As we came nearer, I had to admit it was an awesome cave. I'd never seen one that large except in an old Boy Scout magazine.

"I wonder if someone lives in it," Terri said excitedly. "You know. Like a beach hermit." She cupped her hands around her mouth and called: "Whooooo!"

Sometimes Terri can be such a dork. I mean, if you were living inside a cave, and you heard someone go "whoooo," would *you* answer back?

"Whoooo!" My sister did it again.

"Let's go," I urged.

Then, from inside the cave, a long, low whistle pierced the air.

We stared at each other.

"Whoa! What was that?" Terri whispered. "An owl?"

I swallowed. "I don't think so. Owls are only awake at night."

We heard it again. A long whistle floating out from deep inside the cave.

We exchanged glances. What could it be? A wolf? A coyote?

"I bet Brad and Agatha are wondering where we are," Terri said softly. "Maybe we should go."

"Yeah. Okay." I turned to leave. But stopped when I heard a fluttering sound. From behind the cave. Growing louder.

I shielded my eyes with my hand and squinted up at the sky.

"No!" I grabbed Terri's arm as a shadow swept over us — and an enormous bat swooped down at us, red eyes flashing, its pointed teeth glistening, hissing as it attacked.

3

The bat swooped low. So low, I could feel the air from its fluttering wings.

Terri and I dropped to the hard ground. I covered my head with both hands.

My heart was pounding so loudly, I couldn't hear the fluttering wings.

"Hey — where'd it go?" I heard Terri cry.

I peeped out. I could see the bat spiralling up into the sky. I watched it swoosh and dip beyond us. Then suddenly it went into a wild spin.

It crashed onto the rocks nearby. I could see one black wing flapping weakly in the breeze.

Slowly, I climbed to my feet, my heart still thudding. "What made it drop like that?" I asked in a shaky voice. I started toward it.

Terri held me back. "Stay away. Bats can carry rabies, you know."

"I'm not going to get that close," I told her. "I just want to take a look. I've never seen a real bat close up." I guess you could say that my hobby is science, too. I love studying about all kinds of animals.

"Here. Check it out," I announced, scrambling over the smooth, gray boulders.

"Careful, Jerry," warned Terri. "If you get rabies, you'll get me in trouble."

"Thanks for your concern," I muttered sarcastically.

I stopped about four feet from the bat. "Whoa! I don't believe it!" I cried.

I heard Terri burst out laughing.

It wasn't a bat. It was a kite.

I stared in disbelief. The two red eyes that had seemed so menacing were painted on paper! One of the wings had been ripped to shreds when it crashed on the rocks.

We both bent over to examine the wreckage.

"Look out! It bites!" a boy's voice called from behind us.

Startled, Terri and I leaped back. I turned and saw a boy about our age, standing on a tall rock. He had a ball of string in his hand.

"Ha-ha. Great joke," Terri said sarcastically.

The boy grinned at us, but didn't reply. He stepped closer. I could see that he had freckles across his nose just like me, and brown hair the same shade as mine. He turned back toward the rocks and called, "You can come out now."

Two kids, a girl about our age and a little boy about five, clambered over the rocks. The little boy had light blond hair and blue eyes, and his ears poked out. The girl's hair was auburn, and she wore it in braids. All three of them had the same freckles across their noses.

"Are you all in the same family?" Terri asked them.

The tallest boy, the one who had come out first, nodded his head. "Yeah. We're all Sadlers. I'm Sam. That's Louisa. That's Nat."

"Wow," I said. "We're Sadlers, too." I introduced Terri and myself.

Sam didn't seem impressed. "There're lots of Sadlers around here," he muttered.

We stared at each other for a long moment. They didn't seem very friendly. But then Sam surprised me by asking if I wanted to skip rocks in the water.

We followed Sam to the water's edge.

"Do you live around here?" Terri asked.

Louisa nodded. "What are *you* doing here?" she asked. She sounded suspicious.

"We're visiting our cousins for the month," Terri told her. "They're Sadlers, too. They live in the little cottage just past the lighthouse. Do you know them?"

"Sure," said Louisa without smiling. "This is a small place. Everyone knows everyone else."

15

I found a smooth, flat stone and skipped it across the water. Three skips. Not bad. "What do you do for fun around here?" I asked.

Louisa replied, staring out at the water. "We go blueberry picking, we play games, we come down to the water." She turned to me. "Why? What did you do today?"

"Nothing yet. We just got here," I told her. I grinned. "Except we were attacked by a bat kite."

They laughed.

"I'm going to do gravestone rubbings and collect wildflowers," Terri said.

"There are some beautiful flower patches back in the woods," Louisa told her.

I watched Sam skip a stone across the water. Seven skips.

He turned to me and grinned. "Practice makes perfect."

"It's hard to practice in an apartment building," I muttered.

"Huh?" Sam said.

"We live in Hoboken," I explained. "In New Jersey. There aren't any ponds in our building."

Terri pointed back at the cave. "Do you ever go exploring in there?" she asked.

Nat gasped. Sam and Louisa's faces twisted in surprise. "Are you kidding?" Louisa cried.

"We never go near there," Sam said softly, eyeing his sister.

"Never?" Terri asked.

All three of them shook their heads.

"Why not?" Terri asked. "What's the big deal?"

"Yeah," I demanded. "Why won't you go near the cave?"

Louisa's eyes grew wide. "Do you believe in ghosts?" she asked.

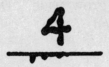

4

"Believe in ghosts? No way!" Terri told her.

I kept my mouth shut. I knew that ghosts weren't supposed to be real. But what if all the scientists were wrong?

There are so many ghost stories from all around the world, how can ghosts *not* be real?

Maybe that's why I sometimes get scared when I am in strange places. I think I *do* believe in ghosts. Of course, I would never admit this to Terri. She is always so scientific. She'd laugh at me forever!

The three Sadler kids had clustered together.

"Come on. Do *you* guys really believe in ghosts?' Terri asked.

Louisa took a step forward. Sam tried to pull her back, but she brushed him off. "If you go near that cave, you might change your mind," she said, narrowing her eyes.

"You mean there are ghosts in there?" I asked.

"What do they do? Come out at night or something?"

Louisa started to reply, but Sam interrupted. "We've got to go now," he said, scooting his brother and sister past us.

"Hey — wait!" I called. "We want to hear about the ghosts!"

They hurried on. I could see Sam yelling angrily at Louisa. I guess he was upset because she mentioned the ghosts.

They disappeared down the beach.

Then, from inside the cave we heard that long, low whistle again.

Terri stared at me.

"It's the wind," I said. I really didn't believe that. Terri didn't believe it, either.

"Why don't we ask Brad and Agatha about the cave?" I suggested.

"Good idea," Terri said. Even *she* looked a little scared now.

Brad and Agatha's cottage was a short walk from the cave. It perched by itself on the edge of the pine forest, looking out toward the lighthouse.

I ran up to the heavy wooden front door and pushed it open. I peered around the tiny front parlor. The old house creaked and groaned as I walked over the sagging floorboards. The ceiling hung so low, I could touch it when I stood on tiptoe.

Terri came up beside me. "Are they here?"

"I don't think so," I answered, looking around.

We stepped past the old sofa and wide stone fireplace and into the cramped kitchen. Off the kitchen stood an old storeroom where I was to sleep. Upstairs was Brad and Agatha's room with a "crawl-through" passage into the space above the storeroom, which would be Terri's room. A tiny back staircase led from Terri's room down to the yard.

Terri turned to the window. "There they are!" she said. "In the garden!"

I could see Brad bent over a tomato stalk. Agatha was hanging some clothes to dry on the clothesline.

We raced out the kitchen door. "Where have you two been?" Agatha demanded. She and Brad both had white, white hair, and their eyes seemed faded and tired. They were so frail and light. Between them I don't think they weighed more than a hundred pounds.

"We explored the beach," I told them.

I knelt down beside Brad. He was missing the top part of two of his fingers on his left hand. He told us they got caught in a wolf trap when he was young.

"We found an old cave in some huge rocks. Have you ever seen it?" I asked.

He gave a little grunt and kept searching for ripe tomatoes.

"It's right by the beach and the big rock jetty," Terri added. "You can't miss it."

Agatha's sheets fluttered on the line. "It's nearly suppertime," she said, ignoring our questions about the cave. "Why don't you come inside and give me a hand, Terri?"

Terri glanced at me and shrugged.

I turned back to Brad. I was about to ask him about the cave again when he handed me the basket of ripe tomatoes. "Take these to Agatha, okay?"

"Sure," I answered, following Terri inside. I set the basket on the small counter. The kitchen was small and narrow. Counter and sink on one side. Stove and refrigerator on the other. Agatha had already put Terri to work in the corner of the living room, setting the table.

"Now Terri, dear," Agatha called from the kitchen, "if it's asters you're after, the best place to find those is in the big meadow down past the lighthouse. Of course they're just coming out about now, so you can take your pick there. I believe that's where you can find plenty of goldenrod, too."

"Great!" Terri called back with her usual enthusiasm. I don't know how she could get so pumped about flowers.

Agatha noticed the basket of tomatoes on the counter. "Oh, gracious! All those tomatoes!" She opened a rattley old drawer and pulled out a small knife. "Why don't you cut these up for a big green salad?"

I must have made a face.

"Don't you like salad?" Agatha asked.

"Not really," I said. "I mean, I'm not a rabbit!"

Agatha laughed. "You're absolutely right," she said. "Why ruin a homegrown tomato with lettuce? We'll have them plain, with maybe a little dressing."

"Sounds good," I grinned, picking up the knife.

I listened to Agatha and Terri discuss wildflowers for a few minutes to see if the subject of the cave would come up again. It didn't. I wondered why my two old cousins didn't want to talk about it.

After dinner Brad pulled out an old deck of playing cards and taught Terri and me how to play whist. It's an old-fashioned card game that I'd never heard of before.

Brad got a kick out of teaching us the rules. He and I played against Terri and Agatha. Every time I got mixed up, which was most of the time, he'd wag his finger back and forth at me. I guess it saved him from having to say anything.

We went to bed after the card game. It was early, but I didn't care. It had been a long day, and I was glad to get some rest. The bed was hard, but I fell asleep as soon as my head hit the scratchy feather pillow.

The next morning Terri and I made our way to the woods to collect plants and wildflowers.

"What is it we're looking for again?" I asked Terri as I kicked aside piles of dead leaves.

"Indian pipe," Terri replied. "It looks like small, pinkish-white bones popping out of the ground. It's also called corpse plant because it lives on the remains of dead plants."

"Yuck." I suddenly remembered the popping hands in my cemetery dream.

Terri laughed. "You should like these plants," she said. "They're a scientific puzzle. They're white because they don't have any chlorophyll. You know. The stuff that makes plants turn green."

"How interesting," I said sarcastically, rolling my eyes.

Terri continued her lecture anyway. "Agatha said Indian pipe only grows in very dark places. They look more like a fungus than a plant."

She dug around for a few minutes. "The weirdest thing about them," she continued, "is if they dry out, they turn black. That's why I want to try pressing a few."

I poked around in the leaves some more. I have

to admit she had me hooked. I love freaks of nature.

I peered up at the heavy leaf canopy above us. "We're definitely as deep into the woods as we can be. Are you sure this is where Agatha said you can find them?"

Terri nodded. She pointed to a huge fallen oak tree. "That's our landmark. Don't lose it."

I started toward the big tree. "Maybe I'll take a closer look over there," I said. "There might be Indian pipe on that dead tree."

I knelt down by the snakelike tree roots and began carefully pushing dead leaves aside. No wildflowers. Just bugs and worms. It was really gross.

I glanced back at Terri. She didn't seem to be having any luck, either.

Then, out of the corner of my eye, I noticed something white sticking out of the ground. I scurried over to examine it.

A short plant stem stuck up from the soft ground. The stem was covered with rolled-up leaves. I tugged at the stem. It didn't come up.

I pulled harder.

The stem rose up a little, bringing a clump of soft dirt with it.

It isn't a stem, I realized. It's some kind of root. A root with leaves.

Weird.

I pulled more of it up from the ground. It was very long, I discovered.

A hard tug. Then another.

Another hard tug of the strange root brought up a huge mound of dirt.

I glanced down into the large hole I had made — and uttered a sharp cry.

"Terri — come here!" I managed to choke out. "I found a skeleton!"

5

"Huh?" Terri raced to my side.

We both stood and stared down at it in silence.

The skeleton I had uncovered lay curled on its side, every bone neatly in place. The empty eye socket in its gray skull gaped up at us.

"Is it a h-human?" Terri stammered in a low whisper.

"Not unless the human has four legs, genius!" I replied.

Terri stared down at it, her mouth open in an O of surprise. "Well, then, what is it?"

"Some kind of large animal," I told her. "Maybe a deer."

I stooped to take a closer look. "No. Not a deer. It has toe bones, not hooves."

I studied the skull, which was fairly large and had sharp incisors or teeth. When I was nine, I had a thing about skeletons. I must have read every book ever written about skeletons.

"My guess is a dog," I announced.

"A dog?" said Terri. "Oh, poor little doggy." She stared at the skeleton. "How do you think it died?"

"Maybe an animal attacked it."

Terri knelt down beside me. "Why would anyone want to eat a dog?"

"They're high in protein!" I joked.

She shoved me hard. "Jerry! I'm serious. What animal around here eats dogs?"

"A wolf maybe. Or a fox," I replied thoughtfully.

"Wouldn't a wolf or fox have crunched a few of the bones and left more of a mess?" Terri asked. "This skeleton is in perfect shape."

"Maybe it died of old age," I suggested. "Or maybe someone buried it here beneath that weird root plant."

"Yeah. Maybe it wasn't attacked by anything," Terri said. I could see the color returning to her face.

We sat silently over the skeleton for a minute, thinking about the dog.

A shrill animal howl made us both jump to our feet. The frightening sound filled the forest, echoing through the trees.

We held our ears as the howling grew louder.

"Wh-what is it? What's making that horrible cry?" Terri shrieked.

I stared back at her. I didn't know.

I only knew it was moving closer.

6

The howls stopped as suddenly as they started.

When I turned around to make sure we were safe, I saw them.

Sam, Nat, and Louisa were huddled behind a nearby tree. Laughing.

I glared at them. I realized instantly that they had been making the howls. Who did they think they were?

It took them a long time to stop laughing. I couldn't believe how much they were enjoying their little joke.

I glanced at Terri. She was blushing. My face felt hot. I guess I was blushing, too.

When they finally stopped laughing, I invited them over to see the skeleton.

Now it was *their* turn to be startled.

Sam's eyes grew wide. Louisa let out a short cry. Nat, the little one, grabbed on to his sister's sleeve and started to whimper.

Terri dug into her jeans pockets for a tissue. "Don't worry," she told Nat. She dabbed at his cheeks with her tissue. "It's not a person skeleton. It's only a dog skeleton."

Those words made Nat burst into tears.

Louisa put her arms around Nat's trembling shoulders. "Shush," she said. "It's all right."

But Nat couldn't calm himself down. "I know what happened to this dog," he sobbed. "A ghost killed it. Dogs can tell if someone's a ghost. Dogs always bark to warn about ghosts."

"Nat," Terri said softly, "there's no such thing as ghosts. They're pretend."

Sam stepped forward, shaking his head. "You're wrong," he told Terri, narrowing his eyes at her. "There are lots of skeletons in these woods. All because of the ghost. He picks the bones clean and leaves them lying here."

"Give me a break, Sam," Terri muttered. "Are you trying to tell us that there's a ghost around here?"

Sam stared back, but didn't reply.

"Well, are you?" Terri demanded.

Suddenly Sam's expression changed. His eyes grew wide with terror. "There it is!" he cried, pointing. "Right behind you!"

7

I let out a shriek and grabbed Terri's arm.

But I knew immediately that I'd been fooled again. When was I going to stop falling for Sam's dumb jokes?

"You two are too easy to scare," Sam said, grinning.

Terri put her hands on her hips and glared at Sam. "How about a truce, guys? These jokes are getting pretty lame."

All eyes were on Sam.

"Yeah. Okay. A truce," he murmured. But he had a grin on his face. I couldn't tell if he meant it or not.

"Sam, tell Jerry and me more about the ghost," Terri demanded. "Were you serious about a ghost killing the dog, or was that one of your fabulous jokes?"

Sam kicked at a clump of dirt. "Maybe some other time," he muttered.

"Some other time? Why not now?" I asked.

Louisa started to say something — but Sam tugged her away. "Let's go," he said sharply. "Now."

Terri's expression changed to confusion. "But I thought —"

Sam stalked off through the trees, dragging Louisa with him. Nat hurried to catch up to them.

"Bye," Louisa called. "See you later."

"Did you see that?" Terri cried. "They really do believe there's a ghost in these woods. They didn't want to talk about it, so they left."

I stared down at the animal skeleton, lying so clean and perfect on the ground.

Picked clean.

Picked clean by a ghost.

The words rolled through my mind.

I stared hard at the jagged teeth in the pale skull. Then I turned away.

"Let's go back to the cottage," I murmured.

We found Brad and Agatha sitting in rocking chairs under a shady tree. Agatha was slicing peaches into a large wooden bowl, and Brad watched her.

"Do you two like peach pie?" Agatha asked.

Terri and I replied that it was one of our favorites.

Agatha smiled. "We'll have it tonight. I don't

know if your dad mentioned it, but peach pie is one of my specialties. So did you find the Indian pipe?"

"Not exactly," I replied. "We found a dog skeleton instead."

Agatha began slicing more quickly, the knife blade slipping over her thumb as the soft peach slices slid into the bowl. "Oh, my," she muttered.

"What kind of an animal would go after a dog?" asked Terri. "Are there wolves or coyotes around here?"

"Never seen any," Brad answered quickly.

"Then how do you explain that skeleton?" I demanded. "It was perfectly arranged, and the bones were picked clean."

Agatha and Brad exchanged a worried glance. "Can't say as I know," said Agatha. *Slice. Slice. Slice.* "Brad? Do you have any ideas?"

Brad rocked back and forth for a minute. "Nope."

Very helpful, Brad, I thought.

"We also met three kids," I said. I told them about Sam, Nat, and Louisa. "They said they know you."

"Yep," Brad replied. "Neighbors."

"They told us a ghost must have killed the dog."

Agatha set down her paring knife and leaned her head back against the chair, laughing softly to herself. "Is that what they said? Oh, my. Those kids were teasing you. They love to make up ghost stories. Especially that oldest boy, Sam."

"That's what I thought," Terri said, glancing at me.

Agatha nodded. "They're nice kids. You should invite them to do something with you some time. Maybe you can all go blueberry picking."

Brad cleared his throat. His pale eyes studied me. "You're too smart to fall for ghost stories, aren't you?"

"Yeah. I guess," I replied uncertainly.

We spent the rest of the afternoon helping Brad weed the garden. Weeding isn't exactly my idea of a thrill. But after Brad showed us which were the good plants and which weren't, Terri and I had fun spearing the bad guys with the special weeding tools he lent us.

We ate the peach pie for dessert that night, and it was delicious. Agatha and Brad wanted to hear all about our school and our friends.

After dinner, Brad challenged us to another game of whist. This time I did much better. Brad only had to wiggle his finger at me a couple of times.

Later, I had a tough time falling asleep. The window of my little room off the kitchen had long, flimsy, white cotton curtains that allowed the light of the full moon to shine onto my face. It felt like staring into a flashlight.

I tried covering my face with the pillow, but I couldn't breathe. Then I tried resting my arm over my eyes, but my arm quickly fell asleep.

I pulled the sheet up over my head. Better.

I closed my eyes. The crickets were making a real racket.

Then I heard something thump against the wall outside. Probably a tree branch, I told myself.

Another thump. I slid a little further down in my bed.

The third time I heard the sound, I took a deep breath, sat up, and tossed off the sheet.

I took a careful look around the room. Nothing. *Nada*. Zip.

I lay back down.

Near the doorway, the floorboards creaked.

I turned to the window.

Behind the curtains, something moved.

Something pale. Ghostly.

The floorboards creaked again as the pale figure moved toward me.

8

I opened my mouth in a low, terrified scream. Then I pulled the sheet back over my head.

The room grew silent. I was trembling all over.

Where was the ghost?

I peeked out from the sheet.

Terri stepped out from behind the curtain. "Gotcha," she whispered.

"You creep," I choked out. "How could you do that to me?"

"Easy," she replied, grinning. "All this ghost talk has you freaked out — hasn't it."

I let out an angry growl, but didn't reply. My heart was still thudding in my chest.

Terri sat down on the edge of the bed. She pulled her robe around her more tightly. "I just couldn't resist," she said, still grinning. "I came down to talk to you, and I saw you lying there with the sheet over your head. It was too tempting."

I glared at her. "Next time pick on someone your own size," I said angrily. "I had the sheet pulled up because I was having trouble falling asleep."

"Me, too," Terri said. "My mattress is really lumpy." She stared out the window. "And, besides, I was thinking about that ghost."

"Hey — you're the one who doesn't believe in them — remember?" I insisted.

"I know. I really *don't* believe in ghosts. But Sam, Louisa, and Nat obviously do."

"So?"

"So I want to find out why. Don't you?"

"Not really. I don't care if I ever see those kids again," I said.

Terri yawned. "Louisa seems nice. Much more friendly than Sam. I think we can get Louisa to tell us more about the ghost if we ask her. She almost told us today."

"Terri, I don't believe you," I replied, pulling the sheet up to my chin. "You heard what Agatha said. Sam likes to make up stories."

"I don't think this is a story," Terri said. "I know I'm supposed to be the scientific one in the family. But I think something strange is going on here, Jerry."

I didn't answer. I was picturing the animal skeleton.

"I'm going to ask them about the ghost again tomorrow," Terri announced.

"How do you know they'll show up?"

Terri grinned. "They always do, don't they? Haven't you noticed? No matter where we are, they always seem to be there." She paused. "Do you think they're following us?"

"I hope not," I said.

Terri laughed. "You're such a wimp."

I threw off the covers. "Am not!"

Terri started tickling me. "Wimp! Wimp! Wimp!"

I grabbed her arm and twisted it behind her. Then I started tickling her back. "Take it back," I said.

"Okay, okay!" she cried. "I didn't mean it."

"And you'll never call me a wimp again?"

"Never!"

As soon as I let go of her arm, she ran to the doorway. "See you in the morning — *wimp!*" she called. She disappeared through the kitchen.

At breakfast the next morning, Agatha asked, "What do you kids have planned for today?"

"A swim, I guess," I replied, glancing at Terri. "Down at the beach."

"Be careful of the tide down there," Brad

warned. "It can sweep a full-grown man off his feet."

Terri and I glanced at each other. I don't think we'd ever heard Brad put two full sentences together before.

"We will," Terri promised. "We'll probably do more wading than swimming."

Agatha handed me a banged-up metal pail. "Might want to pick up some sea urchins or sea stars."

A few minutes later, I took the pail and a couple of old beach towels, and Terri and I headed down the twisty path along the shoreline.

We scrambled up and down the rocks until we came to a spot not far from the sandy beach and the cave.

We slid down the giant rock underneath us and then climbed on all fours across a few smaller rocks until we reached a wide, mossy, tide pool about three feet from the water's edge. The tide pool was about the size of a kiddie pool.

"Wow, Jerry!" Terri exclaimed, staring into the water. "I see tons of stuff in here." She reached into the green, slimy water and pulled out a sea star. "It's so tiny. Not even the size of my palm. Maybe it's a baby."

She turned it over. Its legs wiggled. "Hello, cute little sea star," she sang.

Yuck. "I'll go get the pail, okay?" I said. I

climbed back over the rocks to where we left our things.

Guess who was bent over our stuff? Snooping. "Find anything good?" I called sharply.

Sam glanced up slowly. "I was wondering whose towels these were," he said casually.

Nat and Louisa came bounding over the rocks. "Where's Terri?" Louisa asked.

I motioned toward the water. "Down by the tide pool." I grabbed the pail.

They followed me back down. Terri smiled when she saw us. I could tell she was happy to see Louisa and her brothers. "Look at all the cool stuff I found in here," Terri declared.

Along the smooth surface of a large, flat rock she lined up the baby sea star, two sea urchins, and a hermit crab.

We crowded together to see. Terri held out the sea star. "Aren't its feet cute?" she asked Nat.

He giggled.

We spent a few minutes examining everything. Nat started rattling off everything he'd ever learned about crabs. Louisa finally had to cut him off.

"I want to hear more about the ghost," Terri told Louisa.

"Nothing more to tell," Louisa replied softly. She glanced nervously at Sam.

Had he warned her not to talk about it anymore?

Terri refused to give up. "Where does the ghost live?" she demanded.

Louisa and Sam exchanged glances again.

"Come on, guys. It has to live somewhere!" Terri teased.

Nat gazed toward the beach and the cave. A breeze fluttered his fine, blond hair. He slapped a green fly on his skinny bare arm.

"Does the ghost live on the beach?" Terri asked.

Nat shook his head.

"In the cave?" I guessed.

Nat pinched his lips together.

"I thought so," Terri said. "In the cave." She flashed me a triumphant grin. "What else?"

Nat's face turned red. He hid behind Louisa. "I didn't mean to tell," he whispered.

"It's okay," Louisa told him, petting his hair. She turned to Terri and me. "The ghost is very old. No one has ever seen him come out."

"Louisa!" Sam said sharply. "I really don't think we should talk about this."

"Why not?" Louisa shot back. "They have a right to know."

"But they don't even believe in ghosts," Sam insisted.

"Well, maybe you can change my mind," Terri

replied. "Are you guys sure there's a ghost? Have you really seen it?"

"We've seen the skeletons," Louisa said solemnly.

Nat peeked his head out from behind Louisa's leg. "The ghost comes out during the full moon," he announced.

"We don't know that for sure," Louisa corrected. "He's been in the cave up there forever. Some people say for three hundred years."

"But if you haven't seen him," I said, "how do you *know* he's in the cave?"

"You can see a light flickering," Sam replied.

"A light?" I hooted. "Give me a break! That could be anything. It could be a guy in there with a flashlight."

Louisa shook her head. "It's not that kind of light," she insisted. "It's different from that."

"Well, a flickering light and a dog skeleton aren't enough to convince me," I said. "I think you're just trying to scare us again. This time, I'm not falling for it."

Sam scowled. "No problem," he muttered. "You don't have to believe it. Really."

"Well, I don't," I insisted.

Sam shrugged. "Have fun," he said softly. He led his brother and sister back toward the woods.

As soon as they were out of sight, Terri punched

me in the side. "Jerry, why did you do that? I was just starting to weasel some good stuff out of them."

I shook my head. "Can't you see they're trying to scare us? There's no ghost. It's another dumb joke."

Terri stared hard at me. "I'm not so sure," she murmured.

I gazed up at the enormous black hole of the cave. Despite the morning heat, a chill ran down my back.

Was there an ancient ghost in there?

Did I really want to find out?

Agatha made a really great old-fashioned chicken potpie for dinner. I ate all of mine except for the peas and carrots. I'm not into vegetables.

Terri and I were helping Agatha with the dishes after dinner when she said, "Jerry, I seem to be missing one of the beach towels. Didn't you take two with you this morning?"

"I guess we did," I replied.

"Did we leave one at the beach?" Terri asked.

I tried to remember. "I don't think so. I can go take a look."

"Don't bother," Agatha said. "It's getting dark out. You can look tomorrow."

"I don't mind," I told her. I threw down my dish towel and bolted out the back door before she could say anything else.

I was glad for an excuse to escape. That tiny kitchen was suffocating me. There was hardly any room to turn around in there.

I walked along the path to the water's edge, happy to be alone for a change. Terri is okay, especially for a kid sister. We get along amazingly well. But sometimes I like to be by myself.

I found the big rock where we'd left our towels that morning. No sign of the missing towel. Maybe Sam took it, I thought. Maybe he planned to drape it over his head and jump out at us.

I gazed up at the big cave, dark against the blue-black sky.

"Huh?"

I blinked — and took a step closer.

Was that a light flickering in the cave?

I took another step. It had to be the reflection of the moon, just rising over the pine trees.

No. Not the moon, I realized.

I took another few steps. I couldn't take my eyes off the flickering light, so pale, so ghostly pale, in the black cave opening.

Sam! I told myself. Yes, it's Sam. He's up there right now, lighting matches. Hoping I'll fall for his trick.

Should I climb up there?

44

My sneakers sank into the sand as I took a few more steps toward the cave.

The light glimmered in the cave opening. It hovered so near the entrance. Floating. Flickering. Dancing slowly.

Should I go up there? I asked myself.

Should I?

9

Yes. I had to climb up there.

The light glimmered brighter, as if calling to me.

I took a deep breath, then jumped across a tide pool and over some mossy rocks. Then I started up.

The cave stood high above me, embedded in the boulders. I leaped and scrambled over slippery, small rocks until I reached the next big boulder.

A halo of yellow moonlight shone down on the rocks, making it easy to see. What was it Nat said about the moon? Something about the ghost coming out when it was full?

I scaled the next rock, and kept climbing.

I could see the ghostly light floating above me in the cave entrance.

Up, up I climbed over the scraggly rocks, slippery from the evening dew.

"Oh!" I cried out as I felt my legs give way. A

mini-landslide had started under my feet. Small rocks and sand tumbled down the hill behind me.

Desperately, I grabbed at a fat root growing out between the rocks. I held on long enough to get my footing.

Whew! I took a moment to catch my breath.

Then I pulled myself up onto a sturdy boulder and gazed up to the cave. Now it was right above my head. Only another ten feet or so to go.

I stood up — and gasped.

Whoa! What was that noise behind me?

I stood frozen. Waiting. Listening.

Was someone else there?

Was the ghost there?

I didn't have long to wonder. A cold, clammy hand grabbed my neck.

10

I uttered a choking sound and struggled to turn around.

The cold fingers relaxed their grip. "Ssssh," Terri whispered. "It's me."

I let out an angry growl. "What do you think you're doing?"

"Never mind that," she shot back. "What do you think *you're* doing?"

"I — I'm looking for that beach towel," I stammered.

Terri laughed. "You're looking for a ghost, Jerry. Admit it."

We both raised our eyes to the cave. "Do you see the light?" I whispered.

"Huh? What light?" Terri demanded.

"The light flickering in the cave," I replied impatiently. "What's wrong with you? Do you need glasses?"

"I'm sorry. I don't see any light," Terri insisted. "It's completely dark."

I stared up at the cave opening. Stared up into total darkness.

She was right. The flickering light in the cave had vanished.

As I lay in bed later that night, I tried to use what Mr. Hendrickson, my science teacher, calls my "critical thinking skills." That's when you have to put together whatever facts you have and those you don't, and then draw a logical conclusion.

So I asked myself: What do I know?

I know I saw a light. Then the light went out.

So what was the explanation? An optical illusion? My imagination? Sam?

Outside the window, a dog began to bark.

That's weird, I thought. I hadn't seen any dogs around here before.

I stuffed my pillow over my ears.

The barking grew louder, more emotional. It sounded as if it were right outside my window.

I sat up, listening.

And remembered what Nat had told us. *Dogs recognize ghosts.*

Was that why the dog was barking so excitedly?

Had the dog spotted the ghost?

With a shiver, I climbed out of bed and crept to the window.

I peered down to the ground.

No dog.

I listened.

The barking had stopped.

Crickets chirped. The trees whispered.

"Here, doggy," I called softly.

No reply. I shivered again.

Silence now.

What's going on here? I wondered.

"Sssshhh. You'll scare them," Terri whispered.

The morning sun was still a red ball, low in the sky, as we approached the seagull nest Terri had spotted the day before.

Bird-watching was Terri Sadler Hobby Number Three. Unlike gravestone rubbings and wild-flower collecting, she could do this one back at home, right from our apartment window.

We crouched down to watch. About fifteen feet away, the mother seagull was trying to herd her three babies back into the nest. She squawked noisily and chased them first in one direction, then another.

"Aren't the babies cute?" whispered Terri. "They look like fuzzy gray stuffed animals, don't they?"

"Actually they remind me of rats," I replied.

Terri poked me with her elbow. "Don't be a creep."

We watched them in silence for a few minutes. "So tell me again about the dog barking last night," Terri asked. "I can't believe I didn't hear it."

"There's nothing more to tell," I replied edgily. "When I went to the window, it stopped."

Down the beach I saw the three Sadler kids, in shorts and sleeveless T-shirts, walking barefoot along the shore. I jumped up and started jogging toward them.

"What's your hurry?" Terri called after me.

"I want to tell them about the flickering light," I called back.

"Wait up!" Terri shouted, scrambling after me.

We stumbled along the rocky beach toward the three kids. I saw that Sam was carrying a couple of old fishing poles, and Louisa had a bucket filled with water.

"Hi," Louisa said warmly, setting down the bucket.

"Catch anything?" I asked.

"Nope," Nat replied. "We didn't go fishing yet."

"What's in the bucket, then?" I asked.

Nat reached in and pulled out a small, silver fish. "Bunker. We use 'em for bait."

I leaned down and peered into the pail. Dozens of little silver-gray fish swarmed around inside. "Wow."

"Want to come?" Louisa asked.

Terri and I traded glances. Fishing sounded like fun. And maybe it would give us a chance to ask casually about the light in the cave. "Sure," I said. "Why not?"

We followed them down the sandy path to a shady spot on the water. "We usually have good luck here," Sam announced.

He grabbed a bait fish out of the bucket, then steadied his fishing pole against his leg. He expertly threaded the fish onto the hook, then handed me the pole. The fish flipped back and forth on the hook.

"Want to try?" he asked. I wondered why he was suddenly acting so nice to me now. Had Louisa gotten on his case? Or was he setting me up for another joke?

"Sure, I'll try," I told him. "What do I do?"

Sam showed me how to cast the line out. My first try wasn't great. The line landed about a foot from the shore.

Sam laughed and cast it for me again. "Don't worry," he said, handing the pole back to me. "It takes a lot of practice to learn to cast."

This Sam was certainly different from the Sam we had seen before. Maybe it just takes him a while to get friendly, I told myself.

"Now what do I do?" I asked him.

"Keep casting out and reeling in," he said. "And if you feel a tug, yell."

Sam turned to Terri. "Do you want to try, too?" he asked.

"Of course!" she replied.

Sam started to grab a bunker for Terri from the bucket.

"That's okay," Terri said. "I can do it."

Sam stepped back and let Terri do the honors. I think she must have been showing off. I'd never seen her bait a live fish before. She always hated slimy things.

Terri started to cast out her line without any help. I was about to accuse her again of showing off. But then her fishing line got tangled in the tree branches above us.

That got everyone laughing — especially when the bait fish squirmed off the hook and dropped down into Terri's hair. Terri shrieked, thrashed her arms, and swatted the fish into the water.

Sam collapsed with laughter on the rock. The rest of us laughed, too. We were all sprawled out on a big flat rock.

This seemed a good time to bring up the cave. "Guess what?" I started. "Last night I came down to the beach, and I saw that flickering light you were talking about in the cave."

Sam's smile faded instantly. "You did?"

Louisa's eyes grew wide with concern. "You . . . you didn't go in there, did you? Please say no."

"No, I didn't go inside," I told them.

"It's really dangerous," Louisa said. "You shouldn't climb up there. Really."

"Yeah. Really," Sam quickly agreed. His eyes burned into mine.

I glanced at Terri. I could tell what she was thinking. These three kids really were frightened. They didn't want to admit it. They didn't want to talk about it.

But they were terrified of the cave.

Why?

I only knew one thing for sure: I had to find out.

11

At dinner, we sat at the round table in the living room off the kitchen. Brad was tackling a piece of corn on the cob with his knife, trying to saw off all the little niblets so he could eat them with a fork.

"Brad . . . uh . . . I was wondering about the cave," I started, fiddling with my silverware.

I felt Terri's foot nudge mine under the table.

"What about it?" Brad asked.

"Well . . . uh . . . the strangest thing . . ." I hesitated.

Agatha's head turned sharply. "You didn't go into that cave, did you?"

"No," I replied.

"You really shouldn't go into the cave," she warned. "It isn't safe."

"Well, that's what I wanted to talk about," I continued. I saw that everyone had stopped eating. "Last night when I went to look for the beach towel, there was a light flickering inside the cave. Do you know what it was?"

Brad narrowed his eyes at me. "Just an optical illusion," he said curtly. Then he picked up his corn and began sawing again.

"I don't understand," I told him. "What do you mean?"

Brad patiently put down his corn. "Jerry, did you ever hear of the northern lights? Aurora borealis?"

"Sure," I said. "But . . ."

"That's what that flickering light was," he said, cutting me off. He picked up his corn again.

"Oh," I replied. I turned to Agatha, hoping she'd help fill in the blanks. She did.

"It happens at certain times of the year," she explained. "Something electric gets in the air. The whole sky lights up in streamers."

She reached for the bowl of mashed potatoes. "More potatoes?"

"Sure, thanks." I felt Terri's foot bump me again from across the table. I shook my head at her. Brad and Agatha were wrong. That couldn't have been the northern lights. The light was coming from the cave, not the sky.

Were they mistaken?

Or were they deliberately lying to me?

*   *   *

56

After dinner, Terri and I walked along the beach. Wisps of gray clouds floated over the full moon. Shadows stretched and shifted in front of us as we made our way over the pebbly sand.

"They lied to me," I insisted to Terri, my hands shoved deep into the pockets of my cutoffs. "Brad and Agatha are hiding something. They don't want us to know the truth about the cave."

"They're just worried," my sister replied. "They don't want us to get hurt up there. They feel responsible, and — "

"Terri, look — !" I cried. I pointed up to the cave.

This time Terri saw the flickering light, too.

As we watched it floating above our heads in the cave entrance, the clouds covered the moon and the sky darkened.

"It's not the northern lights," I whispered. "There's someone up there."

"Let's check it out," Terri whispered back.

Before we even realized what we were doing, we were climbing the rocks, pulling ourselves up toward the cave. It felt as if I were being pulled by a magnet.

I had to get closer, close enough to see what was causing that strange, floating light.

Behind us, the ocean waves crashed against the lowest rocks, spraying surf in every direction.

We were almost to the mouth of the cave. I

glanced back and saw that the beach lay far below. In the cave mouth, the light still flickered and floated.

We pulled ourselves up the last few rocks and stood up.

We found ourselves standing on a wide ledge. The dark cave loomed up ahead, towering over us.

I peered into the cave opening. How deep was the cave? I couldn't tell.

Squinting into the dim light, I thought I saw a tunnel leading off to one side.

I took a step closer. Terri moved up close beside me. I could see the fear on her face. She bit her lower lip. "Well?" she asked in a hushed whisper.

"Let's go in," I said.

12

My heart thudded as we stepped into the darkness. Our sneakers slid on the smooth, damp cave floor. I nearly choked on the sour, musty smell.

"Hey —!" I cried out as Terri grabbed my arm.

"The light — look!" she whispered.

It flickered near the back of the cave.

Staying close together, we took a few steps toward it. Our sneakers squished loudly. The air grew warmer.

"It — it's a tunnel," I stammered.

The cave narrowed, then curved away. The dim light flickered from around the corner, from somewhere deeper in the cave.

I swallowed hard. "Let's just go a little farther," I urged.

Terri lingered behind me. "That tunnel looks creepy," she uttered in a tiny voice.

I heard a soft chittering sound somewhere up ahead.

"We've come this far," I urged. "Might as well go just a little bit farther."

Following the light, we lowered our heads and stepped into the tunnel. I could hear the *drip drip drip* of water nearby. The air grew even warmer, steamy.

The tunnel curved, then suddenly widened into a deep, round chamber.

I stopped as I heard the chittering sound again. A soft flapping, fluttering sound. Growing louder.

"What's that noise?" Terri cried. Her shrill voice echoed against the cave walls.

Before I could answer, the fluttering became a deafening clatter.

"Nooooo!" My cry was drowned out by the horrifying roar.

I raised my eyes in time to see the black cave ceiling crumble and fall over us.

13

"Noooooo!"

I was still wailing as I hit the wet cave floor. I covered my head with both hands.

And waited. Waited for the crashing pain.

The clatter swirled over me. A shrill whistle rose up over the sound.

My heart thudding, I raised my eyes — and saw the bats.

Thousands of black bats, flapping and fluttering, swooping back and forth across the chamber, darting low, then twisting away.

The ceiling hadn't fallen.

By entering their chamber, Terri and I had awakened the bats. They whistled and hissed as they swooped wildly over our heads.

"L-let's get out of here!" I cried, helping Terri to her feet. "I hate bats!"

"This is why Brad and Agatha warned us

away," Terri cried, shouting over the roar of fluttering wings.

We both turned to leave. But the flickering light at the far end of the chamber made me stop.

Just a few feet farther. If we made our way a few feet deeper into the chamber, we could solve the mystery.

And never have to think about this frightening cave again.

"Come on," I shouted. I grabbed Terri's hand and tugged.

The bats swooped and darted over our heads, chittering and whistling. We ducked our heads as we ran under them.

To the back wall of the chamber. Into another narrow, curving tunnel. I pressed my back against the tunnel wall and edged forward, still holding Terri's hand.

The pale light grew brighter.

We were getting close.

The tunnel opened into another large chamber, about the same size as the first chamber. Terri and I had to shield our eyes. The entrance glowed with a bright, flickering light.

I took a few slow steps in, giving my eyes a chance to adjust to the light.

Then I saw them.

Candles. Dozens of short white candles perched around the chamber on rock ledges.

All of them lighted. All of them flickering.

"So that explains it," I whispered. "Flickering candlelight."

"It doesn't explain anything!" Terri protested, shadows dancing over her pale face. "Who put the candles here?"

We both saw the man at the same time.

An old man with long, stringy, white hair and a beaklike nose. He sat hunched over a crude table made from a log of driftwood.

Pale and terribly thin, his worn shirt hung loosely on him. His eyes were closed. Shadows played over him. He seemed to flicker in and out with the candlelight.

As if he were part of the light.

Part of the ghostly light.

Terri and I froze, staring at him. Did he see us? Was he alive?

Was he a ghost?

His eyes opened. Large, dark eyes sunk deep in their sockets.

He turned to us, stared back at us with those frightening sunken eyes.

Slowly he curled a bony, gnarled finger. "Come here." His voice was a dry whisper. Dry as death.

And before we could move, he rose up from the chair and began to come for us.

14

I wanted to run. But my feet felt glued to the floor.

As if the ghostly figure were holding me there, keeping me from escaping.

Terri let out a low cry. She bumped me from behind.

I think she had stumbled. But her bump got us both moving.

I took one last glance back at the pale, flickering figure. His bony frame shimmered in the eerie candlelight.

He started toward us, his mouth twisted into a strange grin. The dark eyes gazed at us blankly, like black buttons on a snowman.

Then we turned and ran.

Terri sprinted ahead of me through the tunnel, her sneakers slapping the wet floor. Slipping and stumbling, I struggled to keep up with her.

My legs felt as if they weighed a thousand

pounds. The blood pulsed so hard at my temples,
I thought my head might explode.

"Go! Go! Go!" I shouted all the way.

I turned and glanced back.

He was coming after us!

"Noooo!" I screamed.

I shouldn't have turned back.

I stumbled over a jagged rock — and went
sprawling on the hard floor.

I landed hard on my elbows and knees.

Gasping for breath, I spun around.

In time to see the ghost's bony hands reach out
for my throat.

15

I let out a terrified howl, scrambled to my feet, and lurched away from his bony, outstretched hands.

A few feet up ahead, Terri watched in horror, her mouth open, her eyes wide with fright.

I heard the ghost groan as he reached out with both arms.

Somehow I found the strength to run.

Terri and I were both running now. Through the narrow, curving tunnel. Through the bat chamber, silent and empty now.

To the mouth of the cave.

And then we were slipping and sliding, scrambling down the dew-wet boulders. Down, down to the rocky, moonlit beach.

I turned back once. I couldn't help it.

The cave opening was dark now, I saw. Darker than the night sky.

We ran along the shore, then turned into the

woods. We were both breathing hard, panting loudly as we reached the cottage.

I pushed open the door, stumbled in after Terri, then slammed it hard behind us.

"Terri? Jerry? Is that you?" Agatha's voice floated from the kitchen. She came in, wiping her hands on a checkered dish towel. "Well?" she demanded. "Did you find it?"

"Huh?" I gaped at her, still struggling to catch my breath.

Did we find the ghost?

Is that what Agatha was asking?

"Did you find it?" Agatha repeated. "Did you find the beach towel?"

She stared at us in bewilderment as Terri and I burst out in relieved laughter.

I couldn't get to sleep that night. I kept picturing the ghost. His stringy, white hair. His sunken eyes. His bony fingers reaching out for me.

And I kept wondering if Terri and I had done the right thing by not telling Agatha and Brad about him.

"We'll only get in trouble for going into the cave," I had told my sister.

"They probably won't believe us anyway," Terri added.

"And why should we get them upset?" I said.

67

"They've been so nice to us. And we went into the cave when they told us not to."

So we hadn't told them about the frightening ghost surrounded by candles in the creepy cave.

And now as I lay in bed, tossing and turning, my mind tossed and turned, too. And I wondered if Terri and I should confess to our cousins what we had done and seen.

Despite the summer heat, I pulled the covers up to my chin and stared at the window. Behind the billowing curtains, pale white moonlight shimmered brightly.

The moonlight didn't cheer me. It reminded me of the ghost's pale skin.

Suddenly, my troubled thoughts were interrupted by a soft tapping.

Tap tap. Tap tap tap.

I sat up quickly.

The sound was repeated. *Tap tap. Tap tap tap.*

And then I heard a ghostly whisper: *"Come here."*

Tap tap tap.

"Come here."

And I knew that the ghost had followed me home.

16

"Come here."

Sitting up in bed, rigid with fear, I stared help-lessly as a face rose up in the moonlit window.

First I saw a pale tuft of hair. Then a broad forehead. A pair of dark eyes, gleaming blue in the bright light.

Nat!

He grinned at me through the window.

"Nat! It's you!" I cried gratefully, jumping out of bed, pulling my robe over my pajamas, and lurching to the open window.

He giggled.

I peered out. Sam had Nat on his shoulders and was lowering him to the ground. Louisa, in white tennis shorts and a loose-fitting gray sweater, stood beside them.

"Wh-what are you guys doing out here?" I stammered. "You scared me to death."

"We weren't trying to scare you," Sam replied,

his hands on Nat's slender shoulders. "We saw you and your sister running on the beach. We wondered what happened."

"You won't believe it!" I exclaimed.

I realized that my voice was probably carrying up to Brad and Agatha's room. I didn't want to wake them.

I motioned to the three kids. "Come into my room. We can talk in here."

Sam lifted Nat up to the windowsill. I pulled him in. Then the other two climbed in after him.

They sat down on the bed. I paced excitedly in front of them.

"Terri and I went into the cave," I told them in a low voice. "We saw the ghost. He was sitting in a back chamber filled with candles."

All three of them showed surprise on their faces.

"He was very old and scary-looking," I continued. "He didn't walk. He kind of floated. When he saw us, he started to chase us. I fell, and he nearly grabbed me. But I got away."

"Wow," Sam muttered. The other two continued to stare at me in amazement.

"Then what?" Nat asked.

"Then we ran back here as fast as we could," I told him. "That's it."

They stared at me for a long moment. I tried

70

to figure out what they were thinking. Did they believe me?

Finally, Sam climbed off the bed and walked to the window. "We didn't want you to know about the ghost," he said softly, tossing back his brown hair.

"Why not?" I demanded.

Sam hesitated. "We didn't want to scare you."

I let out a scornful laugh. "You scared Terri and me just about every time we saw you."

"That was just for fun," Sam explained. "But we knew if you found out about the ghost . . ." His voice trailed off.

"Have you seen him, too?" I asked, pulling my robe tighter around me.

All three of them nodded.

"We stay away from there," Nat told me, scratching his arm. "The ghost is too scary."

"He's really dangerous," Louisa revealed. "I think he wants to kill us all." Her eyes locked on mine. "Even you. You and Terri."

I shuddered. "Why? Terri and I didn't do anything to him."

"It doesn't matter. Nobody's safe," Sam said softly, glancing nervously out the window. "You saw the skeleton in the woods, right? That's what the ghost will do to you if he catches you."

I shuddered again. I was really scared now.

"There's a way to get rid of the ghost," Louisa said, breaking into my troubled thoughts. She was nervously clasping and unclasping her hands in her lap. "But we need your help," she continued. "We can't do it without you and Terri."

I swallowed hard. "What can Terri and I do?" I asked.

Before she could answer, we heard creaking above our heads. Voices.

Had we awakened Agatha and Brad?

Louisa and her two brothers hurried to the window and lowered themselves to the ground. "Meet us at the beach — tomorrow morning," Sam instructed.

I stood at the window and watched them disappear into the woods.

The room fell quiet again. The curtains fluttered gently. I stared out into the gently swaying pine trees.

How can Terri and I help to get rid of an ancient ghost? I wondered.

What can *we* do?

17

I woke up the next morning to the sound of rain. I jumped out of bed and ran to the window. The rain swirled in a gusting wind. In the garden, narrow rivulets of water had formed between the vegetable rows and trickled off into the yard. A thick fog had settled on the trees.

"Do you believe this weather?" Terri asked, coming into my room.

I spun away from the window. "Terri — listen. I have something to tell you." I told her about my late-night talk with the three Sadlers.

When I finished, Terri stared out the window. "So what do we do now? How can we meet them on the beach if it's raining this hard?"

"We can't," I said. "We have to wait till it stops."

"I hate suspense!" Terri moaned. She hurried back to her room to get dressed.

I pulled on my old faded jeans, torn at both

73

knees, and a gray sweatshirt, and hurried to join everyone for breakfast. Agatha cooked us oatmeal with big lumps of brown sugar and butter on top.

After breakfast Brad built a big cozy fire and Terri worked on her wildflower collection on the floor in front of the fireplace.

While Terri glued dried flower samples onto sheets of cardboard, I sat around and waited for the rain to stop. Stupid rain.

The sun didn't come out until after lunch. As soon as we could get away, Terri and I hurried to the beach.

We waited there for nearly an hour. I practiced skipping stones, and Terri scrounged around for shells. No sign of Sam, Nat, and Louisa.

"Now what?" I asked, kicking at a small rock. The whole day had been a big waste.

"I brought my gravestone-rubbing stuff," Terri replied. "Let's go over to the cemetery."

We made our way to the small graveyard, climbed over the old stone wall, and took a good look around. The graves were so old. Many of the gravestones had been knocked over, or broken, or covered with weeds.

The forest had started taking over. A couple of big trees had sprouted on top of graves, and one giant tree had crashed across the wall, knocking over several tombstones.

"I'm going to look for something interesting by that big fallen tree," Terri announced.

Terri ran ahead, and I poked along at my own speed. The last time we were here, we stuck to the edge of the cemetery. Now I made my way into the middle.

I started reading the names on the tombstones. The first one I stopped at read: HERE LIES THE BODY OF MARTIN SADLER.

That's strange, I thought. Another Sadler. I remembered that Sam had told us Sadler was a common name around here. Maybe this was the Sadler family section or something.

The gravestone next to Martin Sadler belonged to Mary Sadler, his wife. Then a couple of Sadler kids, Sarah and Miles.

I moved to the next row and continued reading the inscriptions. Another Sadler. This one was named Peter. Beside Peter lay Miriam Sadler.

Whoa! I thought, starting to get the creeps. Didn't anyone else ever die around here?

I moved to another section. All Sadlers, too. Hiram, Margaret, Constance, Charity . . .

Was this a whole cemetery of Sadlers?

Terri's scream cut through the air. "Jerry! Come here!"

I found her near the fallen pine tree. Her face was twisted in confusion. "Look!" she instructed, pointing to a cluster of gravestones at her feet.

I lowered my glance to two large stones. THOMAS SADLER, DIED FEBRUARY 18, 1641, and PRISCILLA SADLER, WIFE OF THOMAS. DIED MARCH 5, 1641.

"Yeah, I know," I told Terri. "The whole cemetery is filled with Sadlers. Creepy, huh?"

"No. No. Check out the kids' graves," Terri said impatiently.

I saw three small, identical stones lined up beside the parents. The three stones stood up straight. They were clean and easy to read. As if someone had taken care of them.

I hunched down to read the names. "Sam Sadler, son of Thomas and Priscilla."

I straightened back up. "So?"

"Read the next one," Terri instructed.

I lowered myself again. "Louisa Sadler."

"Uh-oh," I murmured. "I bet I can guess the last name."

"I bet you can, too," Terri replied in a trembling whisper.

My eyes moved to the last marker. "Here lies Nat Sadler, who died in his fifth year of life."

18

I stared at the three stones until they blurred before my eyes.

Three stones. Three kids.

Sam, Louisa, and Nat.

All dead in the early 1600s.

"I don't get it," I murmured. I felt dizzy as I climbed to my feet. "I just don't get it."

"We have to ask Brad and Agatha about this," Terri said. "This is just too weird!"

We ran back to the cottage. I kept seeing those three stones as we ran.

Sam, Louisa, and Nat.

We found Brad and Agatha out back, under the trees in their matching rocking chairs.

Agatha laughed as we came running up to them breathlessly. "You kids run everywhere, don't you? Wish I had your pep."

"We were in the cemetery," I blurted out. "We have to ask you about something."

She raised her eyebrows. "Oh? Were you working on gravestone rubbings?"

"We didn't get that far," Terri told her. "We were reading the stones. They were all Sadlers. All of them."

Agatha's chair rocked back and forth steadily. She nodded, but didn't say anything.

"You know those kids we met on the beach?" I broke in. "Well, we found tombstones for Sam, Louisa, and Nat Sadler. They died in 1640-something. But those are the same names as the kids we met!"

Agatha and Brad rocked in unison. Back and forth. Back and forth. Agatha smiled up at me. "Well, what's your question, Jerry?"

"How come there are so many Sadlers in that graveyard?" I asked. "And how come those stones have our friends' names on them?"

"Good questions," Brad muttered quietly.

Agatha smiled. "It's nice to see you're both so observant. Sit down. It's sort of a long story."

Terri and I dropped down onto the grass. "Tell us," I urged impatiently.

Agatha took a deep breath and began. "Well, in the winter of 1641, a large group of Sadlers, practically the whole family, sailed from England and settled here. They were Pilgrims who came to start a new life."

She glanced at Brad, who continued to rock,

staring out at the shimmering trees. "It was one of the worst winters in history," Agatha continued. "And, sadly, tragically, the Sadlers were unprepared for the cold. They died, one by one, and were buried in the little cemetery. By 1642, there were almost none left."

Brad tsk-tsked and shook his head.

Agatha, rocking in a steady rhythm, continued. "Your friends Sam, Nat, and Louisa are your distant cousins. Like Brad and me. They were named for their ancestors, the children buried in the cemetery. We were named for our ancestors, too. You'll find gravestones for an Agatha and Bradford Sadler in the cemetery, too."

"We will?" Terri cried.

Agatha nodded solemnly. "That's right. But your cousin and I aren't quite ready for the boneyard, yet. Are we, Brad?"

Brad shook his head. "No, ma'am!" he replied, grinning.

Terri and I laughed.

Relieved laughter.

I was so glad there was a good explanation for what we had seen. I suddenly felt tempted to tell Brad and Agatha about the ghost in the cave.

But Terri started talking about wildflowers, and I settled onto the grass and kept my thoughts to myself.

*   *   *

79

We finally ran into Sam, Louisa, and Nat on the beach the next morning.

"Where were you guys?" I asked. "We waited for you here all afternoon."

"Hey, give us a break," Sam protested. "It was raining. We weren't allowed outside."

"We were at the little graveyard yesterday," Terri told them. "We saw three old gravestones with your names on them."

Louisa and Sam exchanged glances. "Those are our ancestors," Sam said. "We were named after them."

"Jerry said you have a plan to get rid of the ghost," Terri broke in. My sister always likes to get down to business.

"We do," Sam said, his expression turning serious. "Come with us." He began walking quickly over the pebbly sand toward the cave.

I hurried to catch up. "Whoa! Where are we going? I'm not climbing back inside that cave again. No way!" I cried.

"Me either," Terri agreed. "Being chased once by a ghost was enough for me."

Sam's hazel eyes locked on mine. "You don't have to go into the cave again. I promise."

He led us to the rocks below the cave. I gazed up, shielding my eyes against the bright sunlight.

The cave looked a little less frightening in the

daytime. The smooth, white stone gleamed. The dark entrance didn't seem as deep and forbidding.

Sam pointed up at the mouth. "See all those big rocks piled on top of the cave?"

I squinted. "What about them?"

"All you have to do is climb up there and push those rocks down. The rocks will cover the mouth of the cave, and the old ghost will be trapped inside forever."

Terri and I stared at the enormous, white rocks. Each one must have weighed about two hundred pounds. "You're kidding, right?" I said.

Louisa shook her head. "We're very serious," she murmured.

"We cover the cave mouth with rocks?" I repeated, staring up at it. The dark hole seemed to stare back at me like a giant, black eye. "And that will keep the ghost inside? What will stop him from floating out? He's a ghost, remember. He can float right through the rocks."

"No, he can't," Louisa explained. "The old legends say that the cave is a sanctuary. That means that if something evil gets trapped inside, it can't escape through the ancient rocks. The ghost will be trapped inside forever."

Terri frowned. "So why didn't *you* ever go up and push the rocks down?"

"We're too scared," Nat blurted out.

"If we mess up, the ghost could come after us," Sam said. "We live here. He could find our house — and get revenge."

"We've been waiting for outsiders to come help us," Louisa added, gazing at me with pleading eyes. "We've been waiting for someone we could trust."

"But what about us?" I demanded. "If we try to trap the ghost tonight and we mess up, won't he come out looking for us?"

"We won't mess up," Sam replied solemnly. "We'll all work together. If the ghost comes out, Nat, Louisa, and I will distract him. We won't let him see that you're up on top."

"Will you help us? Please?" Louisa begged. "Our whole lives, the old ghost has terrified us."

"You would make everyone around here happy if you agreed to help trap him," Sam added.

I hesitated. So many things could go wrong.

What if the rocks wouldn't budge? What if the ghost floated out and found Terri and me up there? What if one of us slipped and fell off the top of the cave?

No, I decided. No way. We can't do it. It's just too risky.

I turned to tell them my decision.

"Of course we'll help you," I heard Terri say.

19

We spent the afternoon picking blueberries with Agatha. Then we made blueberry ice cream using an old-fashioned churn. It tasted better than any ice cream I'd ever eaten. Agatha said it was because we picked the blueberries ourselves.

As it got closer to suppertime, I started feeling more and more frightened. Were we really going to try to trap a ghost tonight?

Dinnertime finally came. I hardly ate a thing. When Agatha stared at me, I explained I had filled up on ice cream.

After dinner, Terri and I helped Agatha with the dishes. Then Brad insisted on showing me how to tie sailor knots. By this time, my stomach felt more knotted up than Brad's rope!

Finally, Terri and I said we were going to the beach to get some fresh air. And we hurried out to meet our three friends.

It was a clear, cloudless night. Thousands of

stars twinkled overhead. A heavy dew was falling. The full moon made it easy to see without a flashlight.

Terri and I padded in silence along the path down to the beach. Neither of us felt like talking. I kept thinking about Mom and Dad's warning to me before we left home to keep Terri from getting into trouble.

Well, we're in trouble now, I thought grimly. Deep trouble. Both of us.

Maybe all five of us.

Sam, Louisa, and Nat stood waiting at the edge of the shore. The moonlight made the dark water sparkle. I suddenly wished it weren't so bright out. What we were about to do needed darkness.

The knots in my stomach seemed to tighten as I greeted our three friends.

Sam raised a finger to his lips and motioned for us to follow him. Silently, we picked our way across the rocks to the base of the cave.

"Hey — look," I whispered, staring up at the cave. The light flickered brightly in the entrance.

The ghost was home.

I stared up at the cave and planned our route. We'd go up the same way we had the other night. But instead of entering the cave, we'd keep climbing around the side until we reached the top.

Terri fidgeted beside me. "Ready?" I whispered.

She nodded grimly.

"We'll wait down here," Sam whispered. "If the ghost comes out, we'll be ready to distract him. Good luck."

The three of them stood huddled together. Their expressions were tense, frightened. Nat gripped Louisa's hand. "Bye, Terri," he said in a tiny voice. I think he had a little crush on her.

"See you in a few minutes," Terri whispered back to him. "Don't worry, Nat. We'll get rid of that bad ghost. Come on, Jerry."

My legs felt rubbery as Terri and I made our way over the rocks. We climbed steadily. Carefully.

I glanced back at Terri, a few feet behind me. She was breathing hard, her eyes narrowed in concentration.

We reached the mouth of the cave. The light inside shone brightly.

I pointed to our right. Terri nodded. She followed me up the rocks on the side of the cave.

The rocks were damp from the evening dew, and slippery. We were hunched on all fours as we climbed. It was steeper than I had thought.

I struggled to keep from trembling. I knew that one slip could cause a rock slide. The ghost would know something was up.

Hand over hand we climbed.

Carefully. Steadily.

I stopped to catch my breath and gazed down to the beach. Our three friends hadn't moved.

Holding on to a rock with one hand, I waved to them with my other. Nat waved back. The other two remained still, staring up at Terri and me.

I reached the smooth rock surface of the top of the cave. Turning, I held out my hand and helped Terri up onto the narrow ledge.

Together we checked out the situation. The rocks we were supposed to roll over the mouth of the cave weren't as big as I'd thought. They were piled in a solid wall. It didn't seem that difficult to get behind them and push them over.

As I started to move behind the rock wall, I caught a glimpse of our three friends down below. To my surprise, Sam was waving his arms and jumping up and down. Louisa and Nat were also motioning frantically.

"What's wrong?" Terri cried. "Why are they doing that?"

"They're trying to tell us something," I replied, feeling a chill of terror freeze every muscle.

Had the ghost appeared in the cave mouth?

Were Terri and I caught *already*?

I took a deep breath and, ignoring my fear, leaned over the edge to peer down at the mouth of the cave.

No one there.

"Jerry — stand up!" Terri cried. "You'll fall!"

I stood back up and peered down at the three kids. "Hey —!" I cried out as I saw them running to the woods.

A stab of terror made me gasp. "Something's gone wrong," I croaked. "Let's get out of here!"

I turned in time to see the ghost step up behind us.

His entire body shimmered, pale in the bright moonlight. His vacant, sunken eyes glared angrily at us.

He grabbed me by the shoulder and wrapped his other bony hand around Terri's waist.

"Come with me," he said in a dry whisper, a whisper of doom.

20

He dragged us down to the cave entrance.

He's so strong, I thought. So strong for someone old and frail-looking.

The rocks slid under my feet, a gray blur. The ground appeared to tilt and sway. Long shadows seemed to reach out to me, to pull me down.

I tried to cry out, but my breath caught in my throat.

I tried to jerk free of his grasp. But he was too strong for me.

Terri uttered loud, sobbing gasps. She thrashed her arms, struggling to free herself.

But the old ghost held her tightly.

Before I knew it, we were stumbling through the dark, twisting tunnels. The flickering candlelight grew brighter up ahead. We were too frightened to fight him, too frightened to break away.

My shoulder scraped against the narrow tunnel

wall. Terror tightened my throat. I couldn't even cry out from the pain.

The ghost released us as we reached the candle-lit chamber. Glaring at us sternly, he motioned with a bony finger for us to follow him to his drift-wood table.

"Wh-what are you going to do to us?" Terri managed to choke out.

He didn't reply.

He brushed the long, stringy white hair from over his face. Then he motioned for us to sit down on the floor.

I dropped down quickly. My legs were shaking so hard, I was grateful not to have to stand.

I glanced at my sister. Her lower lip was trembling. Her hands were clasped tightly in her lap.

The old ghost cleared his throat. He leaned heavily against the crude table. "You are both in serious trouble," he said in a thin, reedy voice.

"We — we didn't mean to do any harm," I blurted out.

"It is dangerous to get involved with ghosts," he said, ignoring my words.

"We'll go away," I offered desperately. "We'll never come back."

"We didn't mean to disturb you," Terri added in a shrill voice.

His sunken eyes suddenly widened in surprise.

"Me?" A strange smile played across his pale face.

"We won't tell anyone we saw you," I told him.

His smile grew wider. "Me?" he repeated. He leaned forward on the large chunk of driftwood. "*I'm* not a ghost!" he cried. "Your three friends are!"

21

"Huh?" I gaped at the old ghost in disbelief.

His smile faded. "I'm telling you the truth," he said softly, rubbing his pale cheek with a bony hand.

"You're trying to trick us," Terri replied. "Those three kids — "

"They're not kids," the old man interrupted sharply. "They're over 350 years old!"

Terri and I exchanged glances. The blood was pounding so hard at my temples, I couldn't think clearly.

"Allow me to introduce myself," the old man said, lowering himself onto the table edge. His lined face flickered in the shifting candlelight. "I'm Harrison Sadler."

"Another Sadler?" I blurted out.

"We're Sadlers, too!" Terri cried.

"I know," he said softly. He coughed, a dry, hacking cough. "I came here from England quite a while ago," he told us.

"In 1641?" I demanded.

He *is* a ghost, I realized with a shudder.

My question seemed to amuse him. "I haven't been here *that* long," he replied dryly. "After college, I traced my ancestors here. I study ghosts and the occult." He sighed. "It turned out there was plenty to study here."

I stared hard at him, studying him. Could he possibly be telling the truth? Was he human — not a ghost?

Or was this an evil trick?

His black, sunken eyes didn't reveal anything to me.

"Why did you drag us in here?" I demanded, climbing to my knees.

"To warn you," Harrison Sadler replied. "To warn you about the ghosts. You are in great danger here. I have studied them. I have seen their evil."

Terri let out a low cry. I couldn't tell if she believed the old man or not.

I realized that I didn't believe him at all. His story didn't make any sense.

I climbed to my feet. "If you are a scientist studying the occult," I said, "why are you shut up here in this weird cave?"

He slowly raised his hand and motioned toward the shadowy ceiling. "This cave is a sanctuary," he murmured.

Sanctuary? That was the word that Sam had used.

"Once inside this cave," Harrison explained, "ghosts cannot escape through the rocks."

"So that means you are trapped in here," I insisted.

His eyes narrowed at me. "My plan is to trap the ghosts in here," he replied softly. "That is why I stacked the rocks above the entrance. I hope some day to trap them in here forever."

I turned to my sister. She stared thoughtfully at Harrison.

"But why are you *living* here?" I demanded.

"I am safe here," he replied. "The sanctuary keeps me safe. The ghosts cannot surprise me by coming through the rocks. Didn't you wonder why they sent *you* up here instead of coming up themselves?"

"They sent us up here because they're terrified of you!" I shouted, forgetting my fear. "They sent us up here because *you're* the ghost!"

His expression changed. He pushed himself away from the driftwood table and moved quickly toward Terri and me. His deep, sunken eyes glowed like dark coals.

"What are you going to do?" I cried.

22

Harrison took another menacing step toward us. "You don't believe me, do you?" he accused.

Terri and I were too frightened to answer.

"Wh-what are you going to do?" I repeated, my voice tiny and shrill.

He glared at us for a long moment, the candlelight flickering over his pale face. "I'm going to let you go," he said finally.

Terri let out a cry of surprise.

I edged back, toward the tunnel.

"I'm going to let you go," Harrison Sadler repeated. "So that you can examine the east corner of the old graveyard." He waved a bony hand. "Go. Go now. To the graveyard."

"You — you're really letting us go?" I stammered.

"Once you've seen the east corner, you'll come back," Harrison replied mysteriously. "You'll come back."

No way, I thought, my heart pounding.

No way I'll ever come near this frightening cave again.

"Go!" the old ghost cried.

Terri and I spun around and scrambled out of his chamber. Neither of us looked back.

As we hurried out of the cave and down the rocks, I couldn't get Harrison's face out of my mind. I kept picturing his glowing, evil eyes, his long, stringy hair, his yellow teeth when he flashed us that eerie smile. With a shudder, I remembered the inhuman strength of his grip as he dragged Terri and me into his chamber.

I also couldn't stop thinking about Sam, Louisa, and Nat. There was no way they were ghosts. They were our friends. They had tried to warn Terri and me that the ghost was sneaking up behind us.

They said they'd been terrified of Harrison their whole lives. And I remembered Nat's sad face as he told us how much he was scared of ghosts.

Harrison Sadler is a liar, I thought bitterly.

A 350-year-old ghost of a liar.

Down on the beach, Terri and I stopped to catch our breath. "He — he's so scary!" Terri gasped.

"I couldn't believe he let us go," I replied, bending over, pressing my hands against my knees, waiting for the sharp pain in my side to fade.

I searched for our three friends. But they were nowhere to be seen.

"Are we going to the graveyard?" I asked.

"I know what he wants us to see," Terri replied, gazing back up at the dark cave. "I know why he wants us to check out the east corner. That's where we found the gravestones for Louisa, Nat, and Sam."

"Yeah, so?"

"Harrison is just trying to scare us. He thinks if we see the old graves, it will prove to us that Louisa, Nat, and Sam are ghosts."

"But we already know the truth about those old graves," I said.

We stepped off the beach and into the trees. The air grew cooler. Moonlight trickling through the branches overhead made strange shadows stretch across our path.

We reached the cemetery entrance and stopped.

"Might as well check it out," Terri murmured. I followed her through the graveyard, stepping over footstones and loose brush as we made our way to the east corner.

A pale beam of moonlight played over the three old Sadler kids' graves. "See anything strange?" Terri whispered.

My eyes roamed the area. "Nope."

We stepped up to the Sadler kids' graves.

"These look the same as yesterday," I said. "Neat, square . . . whoa!"

Something caught my eye in the corner.

"What's your problem?" Terri demanded.

My eyes struggled to see in the pale light. "I think there's something . . ."

"Huh? Do you see something?" Terri cried.

"Some fresh dirt," I said. "In the corner. On the other side of that fallen tree. It looks like a fresh grave."

"No way," said Terri. "I've checked out all these gravestones. No one's been buried in here for the last fifty years."

We took a couple of steps toward the fallen tree.

"Jerry! You're right! It *is* a grave," Terri whispered. "A fresh grave."

We stepped over the fallen tree trunk, keeping close together. A narrow shaft of moonlight lit up the freshly dug ground.

"It's two graves!" I gasped. "Two fresh graves with little markers on them."

I squatted down to try to read them. Terri moved behind me. "What do they say, Jerry?"

My mouth went dry. I couldn't answer her.

"Jerry? Can you read them?"

"Yes," I finally choked out. "It's us, Terri. The names on these markers read, 'Jerry Sadler and Terri Sadler.' "

23

"Wh-what does this mean?" I stammered.

"Who dug these graves?" Terri asked. "Who put up these markers?"

"Let's get out of here," I urged, grabbing her arm. "Let's go tell Agatha and Brad."

Terri hesitated.

"We *have* to," I insisted. "We have to tell them everything. We should have told them a long time ago."

"Okay," Terri agreed.

I turned to leave — and gasped when I saw the three figures staring at us from the shadows.

Sam stepped quickly over the fallen tree. "Where are you going?" he asked. "What are you doing here?"

Louisa and Nat followed close behind him.

"We — we're going back to the cottage," I told them. "It's late, and — "

"Did you kill the ghost?" Nat demanded. His eyes peered up at me hopefully.

I patted his hair. It felt real. His head was warm. He didn't feel ghostlike at all. He was a real little boy.

Harrison Sadler is a total liar, I thought.

"Did you kill the old ghost?" Nat repeated eagerly.

"No. We couldn't," I told him. Nat let out a disappointed sigh.

"Then how did you get away?" Sam demanded suspiciously.

"We ran away," Terri told him.

It was almost the truth.

"Where *were* you guys?" I demanded.

"Yeah. You didn't do a very good job of distracting him," Terri added sharply.

"We — we tried to warn you," Louisa replied, tugging nervously at a strand of long, auburn hair. "Then we got scared. We ran into the woods and hid."

"When we didn't hear the rocks fall, we got even more scared," Sam added. "We were afraid the ghost got you. We were afraid we would never see you again."

Nat uttered a frightened sob and took Louisa's hand. "We have to kill the ghost," the little guy whimpered. "We have to."

Sam and Louisa tried to comfort their little brother. I gazed down at the two fresh graves. A cool wind made the trees whisper and shake.

I started to ask Sam about the two graves. But he spoke before I had a chance. "Let's try again," he said, staring hard at Terri then me with pleading eyes.

Louisa rested her hands on Nat's tiny shoulders. "Yes," she agreed softly. "Let's go back and try again."

"No way!" I cried. "Terri and I got away from there once. I'm not going back and — "

"But it's the perfect time!" Louisa insisted. "He'll never expect you to come back tonight. We'll catch him completely offguard. It will be a total surprise."

"Please!" Nat begged in a tiny voice.

I opened my mouth, but no sound came out. I couldn't believe they were asking us to do this.

Terri and I had risked our lives by climbing up there. We could have been killed by that lying old ghost. We could look like that horrible dog skeleton right now.

And here they were, asking us to climb right back up there and try again.

It was a ridiculous idea. No way I would agree to it. No way!

"Okay," I heard my sister say. "We'll do it."

Louisa and her brothers burst into happy cheers.

Terri had done it to me again.

24

Terri led the way to the beach. I scrambled to catch up with her. The three Sadlers, talking excitedly among themselves, trailed behind.

The night suddenly seemed darker, as if someone had dimmed the lights. I raised my eyes, searching for the full moon. But it had disappeared behind heavy clouds.

I felt a large raindrop on my shoulder, then another on the top of my head. The wind picked up as we neared the ocean.

"Are you totally crazy?" I whispered to my sister as we made our way over the pebbly sand toward the cave. "How could you agree to do this?"

"We have to solve the mystery," Terri replied, glancing up at the cave. It sat darkly above the rocks. No flickering light. No sign of the old ghost.

"This isn't one of your dumb mystery books," I

told her angrily. "This is real life. We could be in terrible danger."

"We already are," she replied mysteriously. She said something else, but the strong wind off the ocean carried her words away.

The raindrops started to come down faster. Large, heavy drops.

"Stop, Terri," I demanded. "Let's turn back. Let's tell the kids we changed our minds."

She shook her head.

"Let's at least go back to the cottage and tell Agatha and Brad," I pleaded. "We can trap the ghost tomorrow. During the day, maybe . . ."

Terri kept walking. She picked up the pace. "We have to solve the mystery, Jerry," she said again. "Those two fresh graves — they really scared me. I have to find out the truth."

"But, Terri — the truth is, we might get killed!" I cried.

She didn't seem to hear me. I brushed raindrops from my eyebrows. The gusting winds were swirling the rain around us. The rain pattered against the rocks, sounding like sharp drumbeats.

We stopped at the bottom of the rocks. Up above, the cave stood over us, still completely dark.

"We'll wait down here," Sam said. His eyes kept darting up to the cave. I could tell he was really frightened. "This time we'll do a better job of distracting the ghost if he comes out."

"He better not come out," I muttered, lowering my head against the falling rain.

A jagged bolt of white lightning crackled across the sky.

I shivered.

"Come up with us," Terri told the three of them. "You can't help us way down here."

They hung back. I could see the fear on their faces.

"Come up to the cave entrance," Terri urged. "You can always run down the rocks if the ghost appears."

Louisa shook her head. "We're too afraid," she confessed.

"We need your help," Terri insisted. "We don't want the ghost to know we're on top of the cave. Come stand on the ledge in front of the cave. Then — "

"No! He'll hurt us! He'll eat us up!" Nat cried.

"Jerry and I can't go up there again unless you come up to help us," Terri insisted firmly.

Louisa and Sam exchanged frightened glances. Nat clung to Louisa, trembling. The rain swept down harder.

Finally Sam nodded. "Okay. We'll wait for you at the cave mouth."

"We don't mean to be so frightened," Louisa

added. "It's just that we've been afraid of him our whole lives. He — he — " Her voice trailed off.

We turned and started our climb. It was much harder this time. It was so much darker without the moon. Rain kept blowing into my eyes. And the rocks were slippery and wet.

I stumbled twice, fell forward, scraping my knees and elbows. The wet rocks kept sliding under my sneakers, rolling down toward the beach.

Another jagged bolt of lightning stretched across the sky, making the cave glow white above us.

We stopped at the ledge in front of the dark cave mouth. My entire body trembled. From the rain. From the cold. From fear.

"Let's just warm up inside for a moment," Terri suggested.

The three Sadlers clung together. "No, we can't. We're too scared," Louisa replied.

"Just for a second," Terri insisted. "Just to wipe the rain from our eyes. Look — it's coming down in sheets."

She practically shoved Louisa and her brothers into the cave. Nat began to cry. He held on tightly to his sister.

A roar of thunder made us all jump.

This is the dumbest thing I have ever done, I thought, shivering.

I will never forgive Terri for this. Never.

And then a yellow light flared in front of us at the mouth of the cave.

And under the yellow light, the old ghost flickered into view. He carried a flaming torch in one hand. A strange smile played over his pale face.

"Well, well," he uttered in a voice just loud enough to be heard over the rain. "Here we all are."

25

"Nooo!" Nat let out a terrified wail and tried to bury his head in his sister's wet T-shirt. Sam and Louisa froze like statues. The flickering light of the torch revealed expressions of horror on their faces.

Harrison Sadler stood in the cave entrance blocking our escape. His dark, sunken eyes peered from one of us to the next.

Behind him, the rain crashed down, glowing eerily from flashes of bright lightning.

He turned his attention to Terri and me. "You brought the ghosts to me," he said.

"*You're* the ghost!" Sam cried.

Nat wailed, his arms wrapped tightly around Louisa's waist.

"You have terrified people long enough," the old man told the three trembling kids. "More than three hundred years. It is time for you to leave this place. Time for you to rest."

"He's crazy!" Louisa cried to me. "Don't listen to him!"

"Don't let him fool you," Sam added with emotion. "Look at him! Look at his eyes! Look where he lives — all alone in this dark cave! He's the three-hundred-year-old ghost. And he's lying to you!"

"Don't hurt us!" Nat wailed, clinging to Louisa. "Please don't hurt us!"

The rain suddenly slowed. Water splattered off the rocks outside and dripped steadily from the top of the cave. Thunder rumbled, but in the distance. The storm was moving out to sea.

I turned and caught the strangest expression on my sister's face. To my surprise, Terri was actually smiling.

She caught me staring at her. "The solution," she whispered.

And I suddenly realized why she had agreed to come back to this frightening cave, to face the frightening old man again.

Terri wanted to solve the mystery. She *needed* to solve it.

Who was the ghost?

Was it Harrison Sadler? Or was Harrison telling us the truth? Were our three friends the ghosts?

My sister is really crazy, I thought, shaking my head. She risked our lives because she had to solve the mystery.

"Let us go," Sam told the old man, breaking into my thoughts. "Let us go, and we won't tell anyone we saw the ghost."

The torchlight dipped low as a strong gust of wind invaded the cave. Harrison's eyes seemed to grow darker. "I've waited too long to get you here," he said quietly.

Louisa suddenly reached out to Terri. "Help us!" she cried. "You believe us — don't you?"

"You know we're alive, not ghosts," Sam said to me. "Help us get away from him. He's evil, Jerry. We've seen his evil our whole lives."

I turned from Harrison to the three kids.

Who was telling the truth? Who was alive? And who had been dead for over three hundred years?

Harrison's face hovered darkly in the dipping, waving torchlight. He pushed his long, stringy hair off his forehead with his free hand. And then he startled us all by puckering his dry lips and letting out a long, high-pitched whistle.

My heart skipped a beat. I gasped. What was he doing? Why was he making that shrill sound?

He stopped. Then whistled again.

I heard the scraping of footsteps, rapid footsteps on the stone cave floor.

And then a low, dark figure came loping toward us out of the darkness.

26

A monster! I thought.

A ghost monster.

It uttered low, menacing growls as it neared. Its head bobbed low, and two red eyes flared as the creature bounded into the light of the flaming torch.

"Oh!" I cried out as I saw that it was a dog. A long, lean German shepherd.

The dog stopped a few feet in front of us. When it saw Harrison, it bared its teeth. Its growl became a ferocious snarl.

Dogs can recognize ghosts, I remembered.

Dogs can recognize ghosts.

The dog's red eyes caught the light of the torch as it turned to Louisa and her two brothers.

It reared back on its hind legs — and began to howl and bark.

"They're the ghosts!" Harrison Sadler cried triumphantly to Terri and me, pointing.

Snarling, the big dog leaped at Sam.

With a cry of fright, Sam raised both arms to shield himself.

The three kids edged deeper into the cave.

The dog barked fiercely, baring its jagged teeth.

"You — you really are ghosts?" I cried out.

Louisa let out a pained sigh. "We never had a chance to live!" she cried. "The first winter — it was so horrible!" Tears rolled down her cheeks. I saw that Nat was crying, too.

The dog continued to snarl and rage. The three kids backed farther into the dark chamber.

"We sailed here with our parents to start a new life," Sam explained in a trembling voice. "But we all died in the cold. It wasn't fair! It just wasn't fair!"

The rain started up again. The wind blew sheets of water into the cave entrance. The torch flame dipped and nearly blew out.

"We never had a life at all!" Louisa cried.

Thunder roared. The cave seemed to shake. The dog growled and snarled.

And as I stared at the three kids in the wavering light, they began to change.

Their hair dropped off first. It fell in clumps to the cave floor.

And then their skin peeled away, curling up and falling off — until three grinning skulls stared at Terri and me through empty eye sockets.

"Come stay with us, *cousins!*" Louisa's skull whispered. Her bony fingers reached out toward us.

"Join usssss!" Sam hissed. His fleshless jaw slid up and down. "We dug such nice graves for you. So close to ours."

"Play with me," Nat's skull pleaded. "Stay and play with me. I don't want you to go. *Ever!*"

The three ghosts moved toward us, their skeleton hands outstretched, reaching, reaching for Terri and me.

I gasped and stumbled back.

I saw a frightened Harrison stagger back, too.

And then the torch blew out.

27

The torchlight flickered and died.

The heavy darkness made me gasp.

I could feel bodies moving, scraping over the wet stone cave floor.

I could hear the whispered pleas of the three ghosts.

Closer. Closer.

And then a cold hand gripped mine.

I screamed before I heard her whispered voice: "Jerry — run!"

Terri!

Before I could catch my breath, my sister was pulling me through the darkness.

Into the rain. Onto the slippery rock ledge.

"Run! Run!" Terri cried, her eyes wild, her cold hand still gripping mine.

"Run! Run!"

The word became a desperate chant.

"Run! Run!"

But as we struggled to lower ourselves down the rocks, the roar of thunder drowned out Terri's shouts.

The ground shook.

My legs nearly slid out from under me.

I cried out when I realized the roar in my ears wasn't thunder.

Half-blinded by the rain, Terri and I spun around in time to see the rocks topple from the top of the cave.

The rain and wind must have loosened them. And now the big boulders rumbled down, cracking, knocking against each other, bumping, and rolling.

Rock after rock, thudding onto the stone ledge.

Until the dark cave mouth was completely covered.

Shielding my eyes from the rain with both hands, I peered up at the cave, and waited.

Waited to see if anyone would come out.

But no one did.

No ghostly kids.

No old man.

Harrison Sadler had given his life to capture the ghosts.

The cave glimmered white in a flash of lightning.

Now it was my turn to pull Terri away. "Let's go," I pleaded.

But she didn't budge. She stood staring through the rain at the closed-up cave.

"Terri — please. Let's go. It's over," I said, tugging her away. "The mystery is solved. The terror — it's all over."

28

A few minutes later, Agatha threw open the front door of the cottage and rushed out to greet us. "Where were you? Brad and I were worried sick!"

She ushered us in, fussing over us, shaking her head, talking excitedly, glad we were back safe and sound.

Terri and I got dried off and into clean clothes.

The rain had stopped by the time we joined Brad and Agatha in the kitchen for steaming mugs of hot cider. Outside the kitchen window, the wind still blew the trees, sending water cascading down from the leaves.

"Now tell us what happened to you," Brad said. "Agatha and I really were terribly upset that you were out in this storm."

"It's kind of a long story," I told them, warming my hands on the hot cider mug. "I don't know where to start."

"Start at the beginning," Brad said quietly. "That's usually the best place."

Terri and I did our best to tell them the whole story of the three ghostly kids, the old man, and the frightening cave. As we talked, I could see their expressions changing.

I could see how worried they were for Terri and me. And I could see how unhappy they were that we had ignored their wishes and ventured into the cave.

When I finished the story, the room grew quiet. Brad stared out the window at the dripping rainwater on the glass. Agatha cleared her throat, but didn't speak.

"We're really sorry," Terri said, breaking the silence. "I hope you're not angry at us."

"The important thing is that you're both safe and sound," Agatha replied.

She stood up, stepped over to Terri, and gave her a warm hug.

Agatha started toward me, her arms outstretched — when a sound outside made her stop.

Barking. Loud dog barking.

Terri lunged for the back door and pulled it open. "Jerry — look!" she cried. "It's Harrison Sadler's dog. He got out of the cave. He must have followed us here."

I moved to the open doorway. The dog had been

drenched in the rain. Its wet gray fur was matted to its back.

Terri and I reached out to pet the dog.

But to our surprise, it reared back and growled.

"Easy, boy," I said. "You must be really frightened, huh?"

The dog snarled at me and started to bark.

Terri bent down and tried to soothe the animal. But it backed away from her, barking ferociously.

"Whoa!" I cried. "I'm your friend — remember? I'm no ghost!"

Terri turned to me, her expression puzzled. "You're right. We're not ghosts. Why is it carrying on like that?"

I shrugged. "Whoa. Easy, boy. Easy."

The dog ignored my pleas, barking and howling.

I turned back to see Brad and Agatha huddled against the kitchen wall, their faces tight with fear.

"That's only Brad and Agatha," I told the dog. "They're nice people. They won't hurt you."

And then I swallowed hard. My heart began to throb.

I realized why the dog was barking like that. He was barking at Brad and Agatha.

Agatha stepped into the doorway, shaking her finger at the snarling animal. "Bad dog!" she cried. "Bad dog! Now you've given away *our* secret, too!"

Terri gasped. She realized what Agatha was
saying.

Agatha slammed the kitchen door hard and
turned back to Brad. "What a pity that dog had
to show up," she said, shaking her head fretfully.
"Now what do we do with these two kids, Brad?
What do we do with the kids?"

Add *more*

Goosebumps

to your collection . . .
A chilling preview of
what's next from
R.L. STINE

RETURN OF THE MUMMY

3

"Gabe! Gabe! Over here!"

I heard a voice calling my name. Glancing past the angry man, I saw Uncle Ben and Sari. They were waving to me from in front of the reservations counter.

The man's face turned bright red, and he shouted something at me in Arabic. I was glad I couldn't understand him. He kept muttering as he pulled up the hood of his burnoose.

"Sorry about that!" I cried. Then I dodged past him and hurried to greet Uncle Ben and my cousin.

Uncle Ben shook my hand and said, "Welcome to Cairo, Gabe." He was wearing a loose-fitting, white, short-sleeved sportshirt and baggy chinos.

Sari wore faded denim cutoffs and a bright green tank top. She was already laughing at me. A bad start. "Was that a friend of yours?" she teased.

"I — I made a mistake," I confessed. I glanced back. The man was still scowling at me.

"Did you really think that was Daddy?" Sari demanded.

I mumbled a reply. Sari and I were the same age. But I saw that she was still an inch taller than me. She had let her black hair grow. It fell down her back in a single braid.

Her big, dark eyes sparkled excitedly. She *loved* making fun of me.

I told them about my flight as we walked to the baggage area to get my suitcase. I told them how Nancy, the stewardess, kept slipping me bags of peanuts.

"I flew here last week," Sari told me. "The stewardess let *me* sit in First Class. Did you know you can have an ice-cream sundae in First Class?"

No, I didn't know that. I could see that Sari hadn't changed a bit.

She goes to a boarding school in Chicago since Uncle Ben has been spending all of his time in Egypt. Of course she gets straight A's. And she's a champion skier and tennis player.

Sometimes I feel a little sorry for her. Her mom died when Sari was five. And Sari only gets to see her dad on holidays and during the summer.

But as we waited for my suitcase to come out on the conveyor belt, I wasn't feeling sorry for her at all. She was busy bragging about how this pyramid was twice as big as the one I'd been in last summer. And how she'd already been down in it several times, and how she'd take me on a tour — if I wasn't too afraid.

Finally, my bulging, blue suitcase appeared. I lugged it off the conveyor and dropped it at my feet. It weighed a ton!

I tried to lift it, but I could barely budge it.

Sari pushed me out of the way. "Let *me* get that," she insisted. She grabbed the handle, raised the suitcase off the floor, and started off with it.

"Hey — !" I called after her. What a show-off!

Uncle Ben grinned at me. "I think Sari has been working out," he said. He put a hand on my shoulder and led me toward the glass doors. "Let's get to the jeep."

We loaded the suitcase into the back of the jeep, then headed toward the city. "It's been sweltering hot during the day," Uncle Ben told me, mopping his broad forehead with a handkerchief. "And then cool at night."

Traffic crawled on the narrow street. Horns honked constantly. Drivers kept their horns going whether they moved or stopped. The noise was deafening.

"We're not stopping in Cairo," Uncle Ben explained. "We're going straight to the pyramid at Al-Jizah. We're all living in tents out there so we can be close to our work."

"I hope you brought bug spray," Sari complained. "The mosquitoes are as big as frogs!"

"Don't exaggerate," Uncle Ben scolded. "Gabe isn't afraid of a few mosquitoes — are you?"

"No way," I replied quietly.

"How about scorpions?" Sari demanded.

The traffic grew lighter as we left the city behind and headed into the desert. The yellow sand gleamed under the hot afternoon sun. Waves of heat rose up in front of us as the jeep bumped over the narrow, two-lane road.

Before long, a pyramid came into view. Behind the waves of heat off the desert floor, it looked like a wavering mirage. It didn't seem real.

As I stared out at it, my throat tightened with excitement. I had seen the pyramids last summer. But it was still a thrilling sight.

"I can't believe the pyramids are over four thousand years old!" I exclaimed.

"Yeah. That's even older than *me*!" Uncle Ben joked. His expression turned serious. "It fills me with pride every time I see them, Gabe," he admitted. "To think that our ancient ancestors were smart enough and skilled enough to build these marvels."

Uncle Ben was right. I guess the pyramids have

special meaning for me since my family is Egyptian. Both sets of my grandparents came from Egypt. They moved to the United States around 1930. My mom and dad were born in Michigan.

I think of myself as a typical American kid. But there's still something exciting about visiting the country where your ancestors came from.

As we drove nearer, the pyramid appeared to rise up in front of us. Its shadow formed a long, blue triangle over the yellow sand.

Cars and tour buses jammed a small parking lot. I could see a row of saddled camels tethered on one side of the lot. A crowd of tourists stretched across the sand, gazing up at the pyramid, snapping photographs, chatting noisily and pointing.

Uncle Ben turned the jeep onto a narrow side road, and we headed away from the crowd, toward the back of the pyramid. As we drove into the shade, the air suddenly felt cooler.

"I'd *kill* for an ice-cream cone!" Sari wailed. "I've never been so hot in my life."

"Let's not talk about the heat," Uncle Ben replied, sweat dripping down his forehead into his bushy eyebrows. "Let's talk about how happy you are to see your father after so many months."

Sari groaned. "I'd be happier to see you if you were carrying an ice-cream cone."

Uncle Ben laughed.

A khaki-uniformed guard stepped in front of the jeep. Uncle Ben held up a blue ID card. The guard waved us past.

As we followed the road behind the pyramid, a row of low, white canvas tents came into view. "Welcome to the Pyramid Hilton!" Uncle Ben joked. "That's our luxury suite over there." He pointed to the nearest tent.

"It's pretty comfortable," he said, parking the jeep beside the tent. "But the room service is lousy."

"And you have to watch out for scorpions," Sari warned.

She'd say *anything* to try to scare me.

We unloaded my suitcase. Then Uncle Ben led us up to the base of the pyramid.

A camera crew was packing up its equipment. A young man, covered in dust, climbed out of a low entrance dug into one of the limestone squares. He waved to my uncle, then hurried toward the tents.

"One of my people," Uncle Ben muttered. He motioned toward the pyramid. "Well, here you are, Gabe. A long way from Michigan, huh?"

I nodded. "It's amazing," I told him, shielding my eyes to gaze up to the top. "I forgot how much bigger the pyramids look in person."

"Tomorrow I'll take you both down to the tomb," Uncle Ben promised. "You've come at just the right time. We've been digging for months and months. And at long last, we are about to break the seal and enter the tomb itself."

"Wow!" I exclaimed. I wanted to be cool in front of Sari. But I couldn't help it. I was really excited.

"Guess you'll be really famous after you open the tomb, huh, Dad?" Sari asked. She swatted a fly on her arm. "Ow!"

"I'll be so famous, the flies will be afraid to bite you," Uncle Ben replied. "By the way, do you know what they called flies in ancient Egypt?"

Sari and I shook our heads no.

"I don't either!" Uncle Ben said, grinning. One of his dumb jokes. He had an endless supply of them. His expression suddenly changed. "Oh. That reminds me. I have a present for you, Gabe."

"A present?"

"Now, where did I put it?" He dug both hands into the pockets of his baggy chinos.

As he searched, I saw something move behind him. A shadow over my uncle's shoulder, back at the low opening to the pyramid.

I squinted at it.

The shadow moved. A figure stepped out slowly.

At first I thought the sun was playing tricks on my eyes.

But as I squinted harder, I realized that I was seeing correctly.

The figure stepped out from the pyramid — its face was covered in worn, yellowed gauze. So were its arms. And its legs.

I opened my mouth to cry out — but my voice choked in my throat.

And as I struggled to alert my uncle, the mummy stiffly stretched out its arms and came staggering up behind him.

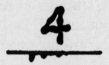

4

I saw Sari's eyes grow wide with fright. She let out a low gasp.

"Uncle Ben — !" I finally managed to scream. "Turn around! It — it — !"

My uncle narrowed his eyes at me, confused.

The mummy staggered closer, its hands reaching out menacingly, about to grab the back of Uncle Ben's neck.

"A *mummy*!" I shrieked.

Uncle Ben spun around. He let out a startled cry. "It walks!" he shouted, pointing at the mummy with a trembling finger. He backed away as the mummy advanced. "It walks!"

"Ohhh." A strange moan escaped Sari's lips.

I turned and started to run.

But then the mummy burst out laughing.

It lowered its yellowed arms. "Boo!" it cried, and laughed again.

I turned and saw that Uncle Ben was laughing,

too. His dark eyes sparkled gleefully. "It walks! It walks!" he repeated, shaking his head. He put his arm around the mummy's shoulder.

I gaped at the two of them, my heart still pounding.

"This is John," Uncle Ben said, enjoying the joke he'd pulled on us. "He's been doing a TV commercial here. For some new kind of stickier bandage."

"Sticky Bird Bandages," John told us. "They're just what your mummy ordered!"

He and Uncle Ben enjoyed another good laugh at that. Then my uncle pointed to the camera crew, packing their equipment into a small van. "They finished for the day. But John agreed to hang around and help me scare you."

Sari rolled her eyes. "Nice try," she said dryly. "You'll have to do better than that, Daddy, to frighten me." And then she added, "Poor Gabe. Did you see his face? He was so freaked out! I thought he was going to spontaneously *combust* or something!"

Uncle Ben and John laughed.

"Hey — no way!" I insisted, feeling my face turn red.

How could Sari *say* that? When the mummy staggered out, I saw her gasp and back away. She was just as scared as I was!

"I heard you scream, too!" I told her. I didn't

mean to sound so whiny.

"I just did that to help them scare you," Sari insisted. She tossed her long braid over her shoulder.

"I've got to run," John said, glancing at his wristwatch. "As soon as we get back to the hotel, I'm going to hit the pool. I may stay underwater for a week!" He gave us a wave of his bandaged hand and went jogging to the van.

Why hadn't I noticed that he was wearing a wristwatch?

I felt like a total dork. "That's it!" I cried angrily to my uncle. "I'm never falling for one of your dumb jokes again! Never!"

He grinned at me and winked. "Want to bet?"

"What about Gabe's present?" Sari asked. "What is it?"

Uncle Ben pulled something out of his pocket and held it up. A pendant on a string. Made of clear orange glass. It gleamed in the bright sunlight.

He handed it to me. I moved it in my hand, feeling its smoothness as I examined it. "What is it?" I asked him. "What kind of glass is this?"

"It isn't glass," he replied. "It's a clear stone called amber." He stepped closer to examine it along with me. "Hold it up and look inside the pendant."

I followed his instructions. I saw a large brown

bug inside. "It looks like some kind of beetle," I said.

"It *is* a beetle," Uncle Ben said, squinting one eye to see it better. "It's an ancient beetle called a *scarab*. It was trapped in the amber four thousand years ago. As you can see, it's perfectly preserved."

"That's really gross," Sari commented, making a face. She slapped Uncle Ben on the back. "Great gift, Dad. A dead bug. Remind me not to let you do our Christmas shopping!"

Uncle Ben laughed. Then he turned back to me. "The scarab was very important to the ancient Egyptians," he said, rolling the amber pendant in his fingers, then dropping it back in my palm. "They believed that scarabs were a symbol of immortality."

I stared at the bug's dark shell, its six prickly legs, perfectly preserved.

"To keep a scarab meant immortality," my uncle continued. "But the bite of a scarab meant instant death."

"Weird," Sari muttered.

"It's great-looking," I told him. "Is it really four thousand years old?"

He nodded. "Wear it around your neck, Gabe. Maybe it still has some of its ancient powers."

I slipped the pendant over my head and adjusted it under my T-shirt. The amber stone felt cool against my skin. "Thanks, Uncle Ben," I said. "It's a great present."

He mopped his sweaty forehead with a wadded-up handkerchief. "Let's go back to the tent and get something cold to drink," he said.

We took a few steps — and then stopped when we saw Sari's face.

Her entire body trembled. Her mouth dropped open as she pointed to my chest.

"Sari — what *is* it?" Uncle Ben cried.

"The s-scarab — " she stammered. "It . . . escaped! I saw it!" She pointed down. "It's there!"

"Huh?" I spun away from her and bent down to find the scarab.

"Ow!" I cried out when I felt a sharp stab of pain on the back of my leg.

And realized the scarab had bitten me.

About the Author

R.L. STINE is the author of over three dozen best-selling thrillers and mysteries for young people. Recent titles for teenagers include *I Saw You That Night!*, *Call Waiting*, *Halloween Night*, *The Dead Girlfriend*, and *The Baby-sitter III*, all published by Scholastic. He is also the author of the *Fear Street* series.

Bob lives in New York City with his wife, Jane, and fourteen-year-old son, Matt.

GET
Goosebumps®
by R.L. Stine

☐ BAB56875-2	**#38 The Abominable Snowman of Pasadena**	$3.99
☐ BAB56876-0	**#39 How I Got My Shrunken Head**	$3.99
☐ BAB56877-9	**#40 Night of the Living Dummy III**	$3.99
☐ BAB56878-7	**#41 Bad Hare Day**	$3.99
☐ BAB56879-5	**#42 Egg Monsters from Mars**	$3.99
☐ BAB56644-X	**Goosebumps 1996 Calendar**	$9.95
☐ BAB62836-4	**Book & Light Set #1: Tales to Give You Goosebumps**	$11.95
☐ BAB26603-9	**Book & Light Set #2: More Tales to Give You Goosebumps**	$11.95
☐ BAB55323-2	**Give Yourself Goosebumps Book #1: Escape from the Carnival of Horrors**	$3.99
☐ BAB56645-8	**Give Yourself Goosebumps Book #2: Tick Tock, You're Dead**	$3.99
☐ BAB56646-6	**Give Yourself Goosebumps Book #3: Trapped in Bat Wing Hall**	$3.99
☐ BAB67318-1	**Give Yourself Goosebumps Book #4: The Deadly Experiments of Dr. Eeek**	$3.99
☐ BAB67319-X	**Give Yourself Goosebumps Book #5: Night in Werewolf Woods**	$3.99
☐ BAB53770-9	**The Goosebumps Monster Blood Pack**	$11.95
☐ BAB50995-0	**The Goosebumps Monster Edition #1**	$12.95
☐ BAB60265-9	**Goosebumps Official Collector's Caps Collecting Kit**	$5.99

Scare me, thrill me, mail me GOOSEBUMPS now!

Available wherever you buy books, or use this order form. Scholastic Inc., P.O. Box 7502, 2931 East McCarty Street, Jefferson City, MO 65102

Please send me the books I have checked above. I am enclosing $_____ (please add $2.00 to cover shipping and handling). Send check or money order — no cash or C.O.D.s please.

Name _____Age _____

Address _____

City _____State/Zip _____

Please allow four to six weeks for delivery. Offer good in the U.S. only. Sorry, mail orders are not available to residents of Canada. Prices subject to change.

GB995